AF242057

Dreams of Gold and Fire

FRED PHILLIPS

Copyright

Published by Raconteur Press, LLC
production@raconteurpress.com
www.raconteurpress.com

Dedication

For my mom, who instilled a love of words at a young age; my son, who unknowingly inspired Aron's optimism; and my wife, who convinced me the story was good enough to send out into the world.

Contents

One

When the shadow first passed over him, Aron had been lying in the grass daydreaming, near dozing in his boredom.

Of all the chores on the farm, watching the sheep in the fields was the most tedious. He'd almost rather be doing anything else, even some of the nastier jobs, instead of sitting here doing nothing. Well, maybe he'd rather do this than deal with the pigs. He was thankful when his father had taken him off that duty and put him in the pasture. Still, the dumb animals milled around in the field, occasionally pulling up a strand of grass and munching on it. That was about as exciting as things got out here.

Every time he complained about it, his father reminded him it was one of the most important duties on their farm.

"The fur and meat of those sheep are what keeps a roof over your head and food in your belly, boy," he'd say. "When you're out here, there's nothing more important in your life. Every sheep that wanders off or is taken by a coyote puts your life in danger. Remember that."

Aron knew the job was vital, but he thought his father exaggerated the importance just a little. He'd inherited the sheep from his older brother when he'd turned ten. In the two years since, he'd never seen a single coyote. And while a sheep would occasionally wander away from the herd, one of the two dogs that patrolled the field usually pushed them back toward the main group. He hadn't once had to draw his bow, call for help, or even move from the spot where he watched. It irked him. Just once, he wanted to see some action in the pasture.

That shadow, though, presented a new wrinkle. He was sure something had blocked out the sun, if just for a moment. He turned his gaze skyward but saw only clouds. Could it have been just one of those covering the light briefly? Aron didn't think so. It had passed too quickly to be a cloud, moved so fast that he'd hardly noticed it.

A big bird, perhaps? He dismissed the thought as silly. None of the birds around here grew big enough to block out the sun, not even the rare eagles that occasionally soared over the field.

An ear-splitting shriek drew his attention above and behind him, toward the tree line at the edge of the field. Whatever was there roared with a fury like nothing he'd ever heard. The sheep in the field bellowed nervously. Aron's heart leaped up into his throat as he scanned the horizon, searching for the source of the scream.

It came again, closer this time. A great wind blew in out of nowhere, whipping the tops of the trees and the grass on the edge of the field like a massive storm. A monstrous creature exploded from behind the cover of the forest, shooting high into the sky, then pausing at the top of its flight and hovering there as if surveying the farm. Sun glinted off jet black scales and huge bat-like wings flapped lazily as the beast circled slowly, eyeing the sheep like they were a dinner table laid for him. He'd dreamed about such creatures his whole life, but his parents had told him he was being silly for even thinking about it. They didn't exist, never had. Yet, here was one right in front of him.

The dragon craned its long, sinuous neck down to stare curiously at him. Their eyes met briefly, then the monster tucked its wings behind it and began a dive toward the field…toward him.

Aron's eyes widened and his knees went weak. For a moment, terror froze him in the spot, but he recovered quickly, reaching for his bow. The sheep bellowed and scattered as the dragon snapped its wings open wide only a few yards above the ground and settled gently into a soft landing. It reared back on its haunches and roared a challenge at Aron. The boy nocked an arrow and let it fly from his bow, though it was little more than a toy to such a beast. The bolt struck squarely in the dragon's chest and bounced away harmlessly, skipping erratically across the ground. Aron fired another quick shot, but it was equally ineffective. He was rewarded by a deep, rumbling noise from the dragon's throat. If he didn't know better, Aron would think it was a chuckle.

Then, the creature leaned forward, placing all four legs on the ground and stalking slowly toward the boy. There was an evil purpose in its eyes as it circled him. Aron looked around in panic. Surely some of the other farm workers had seen the dragon by now, maybe even his father, who often patrolled the fields randomly during the day just to make sure he was doing his job. He expected to see people running and shouting, but no one was coming. Somehow, no one had seen. The only thing in the fields were sheep scrambling madly to get away from the monster who intended to have them for lunch.

He looked back at the dragon. It was close now. Aron knew that he should break and run, try to rouse the farm, maybe even the nearby village. Together, they might be able to find a way to take the beast down. Staring into its eyes, though, he realized that he'd have no chance. It still stalked him, muscles tensed, with a cat-like grace to its movements. The dragon was prepared to pounce at a moment's notice. If he turned to run, it would be on him in an instant, and he would join the sheep as lunch.

Mustering up every ounce of courage in his body, the young shepherd drew the short sword at his waist, barely more than a large knife really, and prepared himself to face the dragon. It was up to Aron to stop it. The beast towered above him now, hot fetid breath pressing down on him, making him want to gag. Its cruel mouth, lined with razor-sharp teeth, seemed to be smiling as it reared its head back. Aron took a defensive stance, raising his sword, and waited for the deadly strike. The dragon's maw zipped toward him faster than he'd imagined possible. He rolled to the side just in time to avoid being swallowed, the keen scales of the beast's jaw scraping against one leg and ripping his pants, barely missing his flesh. His mother was going to kill him, he thought crazily, then he laughed like a madman. What were the odds that she'd get the chance?

As the monster's neck slid past him, he struck an ineffectual blow, his sword skittering off the shimmering scales without leaving so much as a mark. The dragon thrashed its head, catching the broadside of the blade, sending it flying from Aron's grasp, and knocking the boy to his backside.

The sword flipped end over end as it flew and landed in the grass about twenty yards away. He would not get it back before the beast was ready to strike again. As he scrambled around on the ground, searching for anything else he might use as a weapon, his hand closed on the rough wood of the shepherd's staff that he'd never needed to use to keep the sheep in line.

The dragon's head rose above him again, looking down upon his prey. Slimy saliva dripped from its jaws, sizzling as it hit the ground around Aron. Then it opened its mouth wide and struck at him again. As death barreled down toward him, he shoved the staff at it. Amazingly, the shaft caught neatly between the beast's upper and lower jaw. Aron found himself surrounded by teeth and a wet pink tongue, the smell of the beast's breath almost enough to end him on its own. The dragon's mouth was momentarily propped open, and the boy dived away from it. As he rolled to his feet, he heard snapping and popping noises as the monster used the crushing power of its jaws to break the strong oaken staff like a mere twig.

Its roar shook the ground as it angrily reared back for another attack. Aron was out of options. He scanned wildly for any kind of help or anything he could use, but there was nothing. All he could do was stare at those razor teeth as they descended on him for the third, and most likely final, time.

The twang of a bow string awoke him from his reverie, and he looked up just in time to see the shaft of an arrow fly overhead and slam into the neck of a coyote that had snuck out from the edge of the woods. The animal yipped, stumbled, and fell to the ground just yards from the herd. Another shadow—a very real one—fell over Aron then, and he stared up at his father standing above him, looking more dangerous than the dragon he'd just been facing in his daydream. His father dragged him up roughly by his arm, red-faced and sputtering as he scolded him.

"What do you think you're doing, boy?" he yelled. "Didn't you see the coyote? Why didn't you shoot, or at least call for help?"

Aron stood shamefaced as his father vented. He stared at his boots, penitent but unable to form any kind of an answer, knowing nothing he could say would be good enough. Finally, his Da fell silent, staring hard at Aron. When he spoke again, his voice was quiet and cold.

"You were fighting dragons again, weren't you?" he said.

Aron nodded mutely.

"That's the third time this month, and this time it almost cost us part of the flock."

The anger in his father's face made him shrink away. He'd never hit him or his brothers, but Aron had never seen this much rage in that face, either. Seeing his reaction, his father softened, but only a bit, and then he sighed.

"Son, how many times do we have to tell you that there are no such things as dragons? Never have been," he said. "And even if there were, the King's Knights would be the ones to fight them, not farm boys. It's time you accept what you are and make the most of the life you have instead of dreaming about things that will never be."

His father stared at the sky for a moment, then shook his head.

"Round up the flock and get them home. We'll deal with this when your chores are done for the evening."

With that, his father turned and stalked away, leaving

Aron to gather the sheep from the field and lead them back to the pen near the house. He felt silly and ashamed for his daydreams. The one time in two years that he'd actually been needed in the field, he'd been far away. But for all his embarrassment, he felt a small spark of anger as well. His father was wrong about these sheep and this farm being his life. He was wrong about the dragons, too. They all were. They had to be.

He slunk over to the basin in the corner, washing his hands and splashing the tepid water on his face, trying to clear as much of the dirt as he could.

Dusk had settled over the farm by the time Aron got the sheep penned up for the night and turned toward the house. Grime coated him from the dust kicked up by the flock, and his stomach growled from the long day in the field. Even still, he couldn't look forward to dinner. He knew already the disappointment he would see in his parents' eyes. The shame of being caught by his father in the middle of yet another fantasy weighed him down, along with the guilt of almost costing them a sheep.

When he dragged himself through the back door, his mother gave him a quick sympathetic look. Clearly, she'd already heard the story, but she didn't mention it. Instead, she told him to wash up and get ready for dinner.

He slunk over to the basin in the corner, washing his hands and splashing the tepid water on his face, trying to clear as much of the dirt as he could. Behind him, his two younger brothers noisily entered the kitchen and took their seats at the table, laughing and joking. Aron dried his face with the towel his mother kept near the washbasin, thinking maybe things would be all right, but as he pulled it down past his eyes, they met the stern gaze of his father, who had just entered. He crossed to the table and started to pull his chair out.

"No," said his father firmly. "You need to learn a lesson tonight, son. You almost cost us food on the table today, so you need to see what happens when we don't have the animals to provide for us. You won't be eating with us tonight. You need something to think about next time you're in the field. Now, off to your room."

Aron gave his mother a glance, and her eyes held sympathy for him. He could tell that she didn't agree, but neither did she argue with his father. His brothers had gone quiet at the table, their talk of a few minutes ago forgotten with this new development. Aron hung his head and with eyes downcast, headed to his room, recently inherited from his older brother Jonas, who had moved into his own small, neighboring house. Aron knew he deserved the punishment, but he still thought that it was unfair.

He threw himself down on the rickety cot and listened through the thin walls as his brothers and parents enjoyed the evening meal as though nothing had happened. Shortly after, he heard his younger siblings make their way to the mats in the neighboring room that he had shared with them until just a few weeks ago. He heard their whispered conversation as they settled down for bed, as they chatted about this and that so softly, they hoped, their parents wouldn't hear.

Then Aron's attention was drawn back to the other room when he heard his mother speaking in his defense.

"That was harsh, Henry," she said. "You know it."

His father sighed.

"It was at that, I suppose," he said. "I just don't know what to do about that boy, Caroline. At his age, I could run the whole farm. I was providing for my family, not fantasizing about being a knight and fighting dragons."

"Things are different for him. Your pa was gone. You had no choice but to be the man of the family. You never got the chance to be a child, and that's a shame. Thankfully, Aron's life hasn't been so hard as yours. We're still here. Jonas is still here. He has time. He's just being a boy. He'll grow to be the man you expect him to be."

"You keep saying that, but I'm having trouble seeing it. His head is full of dreams. It would be one thing if they were dreams that were possible, but dragons? Half the time, I don't know where he is even when he's sitting right in front of me."

"He'll outgrow the dreams one day," his mother said. "He'll find a nice girl, settle down like his brother, and then he'll be the man you made him."

Before his father could continue the conversation, his mother abruptly changed the subject.

"I talked to Rand the shopkeeper today," she said. "He had a trader just in from the Northern Reaches. They've had more raids—goblins and worse. They think some of the monsters were driven by humans."

His father grunted in disgust.

"It worries me, Henry. What if they make it this far South?"

She dropped her voice then, and Aron had to strain to hear what she said next.

"They took a child on one of the raids. It could be one of ours next."

His father made a noise that Aron couldn't quite hear clearly, but he thought it may have been a deep sigh.

"If the goblins make it here, the King's Knights will come," his father said. "They still protect us. It's as it always has been."

"As it always has been," she echoed. "But there's a new king, and he's across the mountain, far from the raids, with other problems to deal with. It's been years since any king has sent knights to patrol above the mountain. The trader said that the mayor of one of the towns under attack called to the king for help and received a total of three inexperienced knights to patrol the area. None of them knew what to do when the raid came, and two of them didn't survive."

He heard a heavy thunk on the table, his father's hand slamming down on it.

"We've got enough problems of our own, Caroline. We don't need to be borrowing more from the Northern Reaches. It's always been a wild place, and the raids are still a long way from us. If they get closer, King James will deal with them. And if he doesn't, well, we have means of dealing with them ourselves."

His father's chair scraped back from the table and heavy footfalls echoed on the wooden floor as he made his way into their bedroom. Only a few minutes passed before he heard the deep snores of his father's sleep drifting through the walls.

Aron knew he should be asleep. He would have to be up and out to the fields with the sheep just after dawn, and he knew his father would push him hard tomorrow as punishment. But sleep wouldn't come. He kept replaying the final conversation between his parents over and over, thinking about the goblin raids and the absence of the King's

Knights. The people north of the mountain needed someone to protect them. When he became a knight, he'd ask to be assigned here. He'd start up the old patrols. He only remembered them through stories, since he was just a toddler the last time they'd been active. He fancied that he remembered them prancing through the village on their warhorses, armor shining in the sun, but he wasn't sure if those were actual memories or just wishful thinking. Silly dreams, as his father called them.

He would become a knight one day, though. It wasn't silly. He would protect the people north of the mountain—his people.

At that moment, the blanket that served as a door to his room was pushed aside slightly. The light from a candle shone a thin line into the room, and his mother peered in.

"I thought you'd still be awake," she said.

She entered the room, carrying a small wooden bowl in her other hand, which she passed to him. It was filled with the remnants of the night's stew. It was cold, and most of the chunks of meat had been picked out by his father and brothers. As hungry as he was, though, it was marvelous.

"Your father thinks going hungry will teach you a lesson," she said quietly as he shoveled spoonfuls into his mouth. "But I've raised enough children to know that you can't be your best on an empty stomach.

"Your father is a good man, Aron. He can be a hard man at times, but it's only because he wants what's best for his family. He loves you, no matter what you may think."

Aron couldn't argue that point. His father was stern, but he had never been cruel toward his mother or any of them. On those rare occasions when they got away from the farm for a trip to Lanfield over the mountain, he became a different man. Those were some of his best memories, warm and wonderful times. But here, his father expected his word to be law, and he brooked no nonsense.

His mother had told him the story many times over the years, and he was old enough to understand now. Da had grown up hard, Aron's grandfather being killed when he was just eight, a victim of the last round of goblin raids many years ago. As the eldest of three, his father had to take over the duties of the farm even as he grieved the loss of his own father. When it came to making sure his family was safe and had plenty, Aron's father would do whatever it took

Those raids that had taken his grandfather had been the reason for the formation of the knight patrols north of the mountain, but as the years passed with no further troubles, the patrols had dwindled until, finally, they had stopped coming around.

His mother reached over and took the now empty bowl. She patted his hand with a sad smile as she stood to leave. She stopped for a moment before turning to go, staring at him with concerned green eyes that were so much like his own. His three brothers had all inherited their father's stocky build, brown eyes, and dark hair. Only Aron had taken after his mother, with hair the color of straw, a slim frame, and a pale complexion that could burn easily in the field if he wasn't careful. His older brother had often teased him about the resemblance to their mother, and at times, he'd thought it a curse. At this moment, though, it didn't seem like such a bad thing.

"I know you have dreams," she said. "I know what they are. They're the same as they've always been, but it's time to put those aside and start to accept your responsibility here. The King's Knights don't accept farm boys, though I dare say things might be better if they did. The best you could hope for would be the life of a common soldier, and that's not something you would want, or that I would want for you. Better to be a good farmer and live to a ripe old age."

She smiled at him again and left the room silently. The blanket shimmied and danced as she passed, and Aron let out a long, sad sigh.

Live to a ripe old age unless the goblins get you, he thought bitterly as he laid back and tried to sleep.

Aron was demoted to mucking out the pigsty.

Three

Aron awoke to the crowing of the roosters the next morning, bleary-eyed and still tired. It had taken him a long time to get to sleep, costing him hours of rest. Today would be a long day. He quickly threw on his clothes and grabbed the bow out of the corner. He wolfed down the eggs that his mother had cooked for him, noting happily that she'd given him an extra portion. Then he headed out the door toward the sheep pen.

He found his father and his ten-year-old brother Caleb already there. That was unusual, and Aron became immediately uneasy about the situation. His father looked at him sadly and shook his head.

"You won't be needing your bow today," he said. "Go put it in the house. There's not much call for it in the pig pens."

Aron just stared at the man for a moment. His words couldn't have stung more if they'd been accompanied by a slap across the face. His heart sank, but the empty feeling was replaced by a burning resentment as his father spoke again.

"Caleb's taking the sheep today and will have them at least until you can remember what you're supposed to be doing in the fields. You will take his chores, which today, I believe, includes mucking out the pig sties."

His younger brother, at least, had the decency to look embarrassed. Aron turned without a word and took the bow back into the house.

He took his time getting to the pigsty. He muttered to himself as he pulled on the old worn-out muck boots. They were way too big on his feet and slid around, but they only had one pair, so they had to fit anyone who might be going into the pig pens on any given day, whether that be his father or his youngest brother. Or him, sadly. He snatched up a shovel and waded in.

As he closed the gate, he cast a wary eye toward the pigs gathered at the other end of the pen. He searched for the big boar. Alfred, the boys called him, though their father had discouraged naming the animals. When you might have to slaughter one during a hard winter, it was best you didn't get attached, he always said. But the boys ignored their father's advice in a few instances, and Alfred was one of them. They named him after the first king, because he was certainly the ruler of his pen. Alfred was known to be the cranky sort and would at times revert to feral instinct if he felt the need to protect his territory. Today, the boar seemed calm enough when Aron spotted him huddled in the corner with a couple of sows, so he began his work.

Aron soon realized how wrong he'd been yesterday when he thought tending the sheep was the most tedious, boring job on the farm. At least it wasn't disgusting, too. He shoveled mounds of a stinking mixture of mud, feces, and rotten food into pails and hauled them around to the back edge of the farm. In the spring, they'd haul some of it back to be used as fertilizer on their vegetable crops. It was foul, dirty, and hard work, but at least he could let his mind wander while he did it. The pigs were closer to the house than the pasture fields, and weren't in any danger from coyotes. In fact, he pitied any predator that might try to tangle with King Alfred.

He drifted off, thinking about the goblin raids he'd learned about from his parents' conversation the night before. He imagined himself riding at the head of that knightly parade that he thought he remembered from his very youngest days, his armor shining brighter in the sun than anyone else's. He waved to his mother and father and brothers as he and his knights rode by, sitting high and proud in the saddle as they headed out to put the goblins down once again. This time, though, he'd make sure the patrols continued so the folk above the mountain would be protected for as long as he lived and breathed. He would vow it. That's what knights did, right? They made vows and hunted goblins.

As he returned from his second trip at the back of the farm with an armload of empty pails, he imagined the cheers and the laurels that would be bestowed upon him after his glorious victory. He threw the gate open, marching toward the adoring crowd, but his happy reverie was shattered by a wild squeal. He jolted from the daydream to a threat much more real and present than goblins. He stared in horror as King Alfred charged, with nearly 250 pounds of angry boar bearing down on his slight frame. Aron spun to try to get to safety, but one of the oversized boots slid out from under him, sending him sprawling face-first into the nasty muck. He came up spluttering as Alfred darted straight past him, headed for the open gate. The boar blasted through to freedom and was gone.

Aron pulled himself slowly to his feet, looking for a clean piece of cloth anywhere on his body to wipe the stinking slurry off his face. He didn't find one. He noticed a couple of the sows inching toward the open gate and quickly crossed the distance to slam it shut. That's when he heard a deep laugh behind him, a sound that he didn't hear often.

He turned to find his father leaning on the railing of the pen, a huge grin plastered on his face. It would have been a welcome sight if it hadn't been at his expense.

"Well now, son," he said. "Looks like your dragon got the best of you today."

Aron didn't reply, just snatched up his shovel out of the mud and turned back to the work.

"What are you waiting on?" his father asked. "The dragon's getting away. You'd better go catch it."

His father watched the embarrassing spectacle as Aron chased Alfred around the farm, trying to corral him back toward the gate. His older brother Jonas joined his father, and they laughed long and hard at Aron's trials for a good half-hour before they finally gave in and helped him get the boar back into the pen.

When they had King Alfred back in his throne room, Jonas punched him playfully in the shoulder and his father ruffled his nasty hair and said, "think about that the next time you start to daydream." Aron knew his father meant it to be an affectionate gesture, probably as close to an apology for yesterday as he was likely to get, but he wasn't feeling in the mood to accept it at the moment.

"I'd say that's enough for you today," his father said. "Get cleaned up. You can finish the mucking tomorrow."

Stubbornly, Aron picked the shovel up and began the chore again. His father watched him work for a moment, then nodded and walked away. He continued the long hard job for the rest of the afternoon, keeping an eye out for Alfred as he did so. He stewed in his anger. Even though he knew that all was forgiven with his father, all wasn't forgiven with him. His mind was made up. He wouldn't spend the rest of his life shoveling pig dung and watching dumb sheep. He would be a knight. He would be the greatest knight who had ever lived. No matter what it took.

Four

Aron dunked himself in the small stream that ran at the edge of the family property and stripped his foul clothes off before he walked through the door. If he'd tried to enter with the filth of the pig pens covering him, it might have been easier to face a dragon than his mother.

Everyone else was already gathered around the table by the time he'd changed into fresh clothes, anticipation high for a rare treat. Caleb had spotted a few deer on the edge of the pasture and alerted their father, who had managed to stalk one of them with his bow. His mother had rubbed the backstraps with some of the herbs from her garden and roasted it with fall potatoes. It was one of Aron's favorite meals—the best cut of the deer—but he couldn't manage to make himself savor it like he should have. He chewed with little joy, barely tasting what might be the best meal he'd have in a long time. Work on the farm left them precious little opportunity to hunt, so having fresh venison was a special occasion.

Everyone else at the table remained unusually quiet, sensing Aron's mood. He waited for his father to make a joke about what had happened in the pigsty today, but Da didn't mention it at all. Mother tried to keep up a little bit of small talk, and his brothers answered her questions about their day, but even their normal raucous racket was subdued in the uncomfortable environment. The talk around the table should have focused on Caleb's first day tending the sheep, a momentous occasion. When Aron had moved to the pasture, they had celebrated over dinner. No one wanted to bring it up with him there. Well, if no one wanted to make him feel bad, they should have thought about that before they sent him to muck out the pig pens.

As soon as he cleared his plate, Aron headed to his room without a word, sulking in silence. He flopped down on the cot and waited. He would not sleep tonight. He had other things to do.

Shortly after he'd retired, his brothers made their way to their room chattering excitedly. With Aron out of the picture, they had no trouble talking about Caleb's promotion on the farm. The youngest, apparently thinking Aron couldn't hear them through the thin walls and cloth door, asked Caleb about his experience. Caleb happily regaled his younger brother with tall tales of fighting off predators all day to save the sheep. Aron knew the fibs for what they were, but he didn't care. Let his little brother have the spotlight—and the sheep. He was welcome to both.

Not long after, he heard his father head to the bedroom. After twenty minutes or so, the predictable snoring signaled that he was asleep. Mother, as always, retired last. She stopped first to check in on his brothers to make sure they were asleep. Then she gently brushed back the blanket to his room. She quietly called his name, but he pretended to be asleep, and after a moment, she moved on. Once she had gone to bed, he waited. He guessed it was probably no more than an hour, but it felt like an eternity. Unlike his brothers' silence or his father's snoring, his mother would give no clear signal when she was asleep, so he waited a few minutes more just to be sure. Then he sat up on the side of the cot and made his move.

First, he gathered his best clothes—the ones that were reserved for weddings, funerals, and the rare trip to Lanfield. It was the only outfit that had been purchased for him instead of being handed down from his older brother. He wanted to make a good first impression. He carefully folded them and placed them into his worn pack, also a hand-me-down from Jonas. Next, he packed a few of the snares he occasionally set out in the edges of the pasture to catch a rabbit or other small animal for supper, along with his small skinning knife. He paused for a second, remembering a fond afternoon with his father when he'd learned to tie the snares and also how to clean and prepare the rabbits they'd brought home. He shook his head to clear the thought. That was a long time ago, and things had clearly changed.

On top of that, he added his threadbare cloak. Autumn was near, after all, and the nights may get cold on the mountain. Finally, he grabbed the waterskin he used when watching the sheep in the heat of the summer and his bow from the corner. He gingerly pulled the blanket door of his room aside and slipped into the kitchen.

He slowly and quietly eased the larder open, hoping that the hinges wouldn't squeak and give him away. For once, they moved smoothly, for which he was grateful. He took out what he guessed would be enough salt pork to sustain him for the journey south. He would need to survive for maybe three or four days on what he could carry or hunt. The pork wouldn't have been his first choice for meals, but it would fill his belly, be easy to carry, and he didn't have to worry about it going bad. After a moment's thought, he also nicked some of the leftover venison that his mother had set aside for breakfast and wrapped it in one of the small towels. He'd at least have a tasty first meal on the road.

He slipped out the door then, taking extra time and care to close it without a sound. He stopped at the well, filling his waterskin with as much as it would hold and then drinking deeply before moving on. The water he'd find along the way wouldn't be nearly this clean or sweet. He stopped in the shadow of the shed near the pig pen, listening cautiously. He wanted to make sure they didn't notice him, especially King Alfred. They might raise a ruckus that would alert those in the house. The pigs were laid in a pile asleep in the corner. He cracked the shed open and took down the large knife that his father used when they had to slaughter a pig. It certainly wasn't a sword, but it was the closest thing he'd find on the farm.

Well, that wasn't exactly true. Aron knew his father kept a real sword locked in a trunk in their bedroom. His grandfather had used the blade as a soldier in the first goblin incursions, and he'd seen it a few times when his father took it out to oil and inspect the blade. As far as Aron knew, his Da didn't know how to use it, but he kept it spotless and ready. Of course, it might as well have been hidden in a dragon's hoard for all the good it did Aron there. There was no way he could get his hands on it, and even if he could, he doubted he could handle the thing. It was a big, beastly weapon, requiring someone three or four times his size to wield properly. The knife would have to do.

As he made his way to the edge of the property, the only home he'd ever known, Aron stopped and took one last look at the house in the moonlight. He faltered for a moment. He could put everything up, sneak back into his room, and give up on this crazy plan. No one would know the difference. On some level, he knew that his mother had spoken honestly. If he went through with this, likely the best thing that could happen was the captain of the King's Knights laughing at him and sending him home in shame. If things went badly, he might never see this house or his family again. His whole life rode on this one decision, this one moment. He could continue south across the mountain and try to make his dreams come true or he could walk back into the house, fall asleep in his familiar cot, and spend the rest of his life mucking out pig pens and keeping track of stupid sheep.

With uncertain steps, he made his choice. He said farewell to his home and turned down the path that led to the mountain road. He didn't care what everyone else thought. He would become a knight, even if it killed him.

Aron leaves home to become a knight.

Five

As dawn broke, Aron turned to look back toward the small village he'd left behind from a higher vantage point. He nibbled on the last of the venison that he'd taken from the kitchen and watched the first stirrings of life in his old world. Early risers were leaving their homes, heading out for a day's work in the fields surrounding the town. His father and brothers would be among them shortly. It would only be a matter of minutes before they realized he wasn't there. Some of those people would be coming this way soon for a day at the mines, and he couldn't be here when that happened. He needed to put as much distance as possible between the village and himself. He fought fatigue, having climbed the mountain road all night with no sleep, but still he had to push forward.

He faced a three-day journey by foot on the switchbacks over the mountain to Lanfield, the seat of the king, the home of the King's Knights, and the place where he'd find his destiny. On the roads, the trip presented little difficulty.

They were well-traveled, and if not for fear of his father catching up to him, he might even be able to catch a ride on a passing wagon and get there faster. But he wanted no witnesses to point people in his direction. He'd decided it was best to get off the road as much as possible and avoid other travelers. He didn't want to be packed off back home by one of them.

Known as simply The Mountain by the people of his village, it was actually quite a grand name for the peak that Aron now climbed. In truth, it was only the beginning of the range of mountains that stretched back to the west, the peaks there dwarfing the small foothill that lay on the edge of his world. Roads into those mountains branched off from this one, but few people traveled them. Danger lay that way in both the treacherous terrain and the inhabitants along the way. People lived there, but they were strange, not at all like the villagers or even the people of Lanfield. At least, so his neighbors said. He knew of one trader of the mountain tribes who came to the village a couple of times a year. He talked oddly and wore primitive clothing, mostly furs and skins, but he seemed to be a nice enough sort of fellow, and he loved to spin tales for anyone who would listen.

The trader's tales also frightened people. He shared stories of bizarre creatures in the mountains, monsters made of stone, large hairy man-shaped things that could hurl boulders, hunting cats as large as a draft horse, and great serpents that could swallow a man whole. His mother and father scoffed at the wild stories, just as they laughed about his dreams of dragons. But the trader was earnest, and Aron believed that at least some of them were true. Which ones, he couldn't say.

He took one last long look at the roofs of the village. Aron knew that people would be looking for him soon, so it was time to move on. He turned his attention back to the upward slope of the road. If he could keep his legs moving all day, he might make the peak of the mountain by nightfall. The remainder of the trip would be downhill and therefore much easier.

As he walked, he rehearsed over and over in his head the pitch that he would give when he arrived in Lanfield. He'd need to spin a tale worthy of getting to the captain of the King's Knights in the first place. The challenge only began there. Then, he'd have to convince the man to bend the ancient rules of knighthood to allow a farmer's son to join. He knew that it wouldn't be an easy task, but it wasn't like he wanted them to admit him to the King's Guard. He just wanted to protect his home and his family. Surely, they'd understand that.

Aron managed to keep moving through the day, but just barely. By the time the sun sank behind those peaks to the west, exhaustion had overtaken him. He'd made good time despite his weariness and had been able to stay to the road most of the day. He'd had to slip off into the rocks a few times to avoid passing travelers, but most were coming from the direction of Lanfield. He'd kept his singular focus and kept his legs pumping, even though they burned and protested. He would sleep on top of the mountain tonight and start down the other side tomorrow. He might even make Lanfield by nightfall the next day. At the least, he'd enter the city gates early the day after.

The pre-fall wind blew chill at this height, and Aron was glad for the cloak that he'd packed despite its holes and patches. Just off the road, he found a perfect spot to set up camp, beneath an overhanging shelf that was sheltered by brush. He thought briefly about setting out some of the snares in hopes of getting some fresh meat, but he didn't have the energy. His arms and legs felt like the heavy pails full of pig dung that he'd hauled for hours the day before. He didn't even have the desire to try to build a fire, and he'd also realized that he hadn't thought about that need, and had neither flint nor tinder. He realized for the first time how unprepared he was for the path that he'd set himself on and thought again about turning back. He pushed the thought away grumpily.

He nibbled on a bit of the salt pork as he sat in his campsite and also cursed himself for not packing a bedroll or at least a blanket. This would be an uncomfortable night. Aron dragged his pack deep into the crevice under the shelf and laid his head on the lumpy makeshift pillow. He curled up, pulling the cloak as tightly about him as possible. Despite the hard rocky ground and chill air, he was snoring within minutes.

The boy woke the next morning feeling very stiff and sore, but rested nonetheless. He walked around the small opening, stretching painful cramps out of his muscles and warming his limbs after a night spent on the cold ground. He took a couple of pieces of the pork from his pack and checked the canteen. It was getting light, but there was a mountain spring down the road a little way that travelers used. His family had stopped there on almost every trip over the mountain. He could refill there. Shouldering his pack, he set off downhill, gnawing on the meat as he walked.

He kept a quick pace throughout the day, though not as fast as the previous day. It passed uneventfully, if uncomfortably, and he again made good time. He set up camp at the base of the mountain on the second night. He faced a two-hour walk in the morning to the gates of Lanfield, where he would meet his future. It had been a long trek, but tomorrow, he would take his first true step toward becoming a knight.

There were two rough-looking guards manning the entrance.

Six

Despite two uncomfortable nights of sleeping on the ground with no blanket and no fire, there was a spring in Aron's step as he approached the outskirts of Lanfield. He practically skipped down the road, excitement pulsing through him.

As he came closer to the city, he remembered his first trip there only a few years ago. He'd been eight when his father had needed to go to court to settle a particularly contentious land dispute, and had allowed his two oldest sons to tag along. One of their neighbors had died, leaving a son who lived in the city. The son had tried to claim a large chunk of his Da's land as his own. Aron remembered the awe and amazement he'd felt the first time he saw the stone walls of the inner city and the mass of people and shops both inside and outside that wall. He'd visited a few more times since, rendering him a little less awed, but still impressed.

Lanfield was not, Aron had been told, a large city, but he couldn't imagine what a bigger one would look like. The walls of the inner city rose high above the surrounding homes and shops. They were largely a mottled brown, made from many types of stone of varying shades and colors, but at intervals, you could see a snow-white river stone or a colorful piece of rock from the mountains. His father had explained that the walled area had once been the whole of the city, but over the years, it had grown beyond what they could contain. The king's castle stood at the center of the old city, and the rest of the area was taken up with shops and inns that catered to well-to-do visitors who could afford their accommodations. Most of the people who populated the inner city, in fact, were what his father would call rich.

Around the walls a much larger city had sprung up. Here were found the shops and inns that a common person could afford to use. When his family had come to visit, this was where they'd stayed and where they'd bought the few things that couldn't be had in their village. There was a smithy here, and open-air markets where those in the surrounding villages came to sell their produce and wares. Beyond the shops were homes and boarding houses. In short, it contained everything a city needed on its own.

As Aron took his first steps between the buildings of the outer city, he realized how easy it would be for someone to get lost here. People hustled and bustled all about—there was much more activity than he would ever see back home. He spotted a kindly looking man at the edge of the market selling several varieties of fruit, likely grown in his own orchard. Wanting a change from the salt pork he'd had for most of the last two days, he thought he would spend a portion of the few coins he had in his pocket on one of the large, shiny apples.

The ripe, juicy red fruit cost a half-penny, a quarter of his meager fortune, but when he bit into the sweet, crisp meat of it and the sticky juice ran down his chin, he called it worth every bit of what it cost. The farmer struck up a conversation with him, surprised and curious to see a boy his age who was obviously from the villages alone in the market. Aron answered a few of the man's questions, telling him that he'd grown up on a farm, but he was careful not to say too much. The man's curiosity also reeked of suspicion. He didn't think it was possible that word of his disappearance could have beaten him to Lanfield, or that anyone there would care if it had, but he didn't want to take any chances. Finally, after a few minutes of idle chit chat, he asked the question that he really wanted answered.

"Where could I find the Captain of the King's Knights?" he asked.

The old man chuckled and looked at him strangely.

"The Captain doesn't have time for farm boys," he said, unintentionally echoing what Aron's parents had both told him. "Why would you think you could meet him?"

"I intend to join the knighthood."

The man smiled at first, thinking it was a joke. On seeing that Aron was serious, the lines of his face hardened, and he gave him a dark look.

"Take my advice, boy," he said. "Go back home to your farm. Unless you're royalty in disguise, which I doubt, you've got no chance of becoming a knight. At best, they might conscript you into the army and feed you to the front lines as fodder, but if I'm any judge, you're too young and scrawny even for that."

Hearing his parents' words from the mouth of a complete stranger whom he'd just met cut Aron deeply. He ducked his head, and his shoulders sagged. For a moment, he thought the man might be right, and he should just turn around and go home, then he found a resolve within himself. No. He'd come this far. He would see this through, and he would show them all. He puffed up his chest and looked at the man defiantly.

"I'm as good as any royal, and I'll prove it," he said. "No one will work harder to become a knight than me."

The response surprised the merchant, and for a second, he only stared at Aron. Then he sighed and shook his head.

"I don't doubt that at all," he said. "The King's Knights are headquartered inside the walls. It's the nearest building to the castle. If you go through the gates and follow this road straight, you can't miss it. There's a huge banner out front with the crest on it. But you'll never get through the gates. They're guarded, and not just anyone may pass. You must live there or have business there. The gate guards will boot you before you get within a mile of the Captain of the Knights. Save yourself the embarrassment and just go home."

He would not. Aron dug in his heels.

"I've left my family and come over the mountain by foot. I won't go home. I will be a knight."

The man gave him a wry, humorless smile and again shook his head.

"That journey, I'm thinking, will be the least of your trials before this is over. It would be easier for you to move that mountain by hand than to get what you want, but if you're determined to go through with it, good luck. May the gods go with you."

With that, the man turned and busied himself rearranging the fruit that he had for sale, dismissing and ignoring Aron. He stood staring at the merchant's back and once again contemplated the path before him. Then, with only a moment's hesitation, he turned and strode boldly toward the wall.

A short line formed as Aron stood outside one of the less grand gates into the inner city. It stood about ten feet tall and about as wide, enough to pass a coach wagon through, but not much more. There were two rough-looking guards manning the entrance. While they wore armor and swords swung at their waists, they were most certainly not knights, at least not as he'd imagined them. The armor didn't gleam in the sun. In fact, it was quite dull and tarnished. As he got closer, he also realized that hygiene was not the guards' strong point either. The day was warm, and their armor heavy, and they reeked as he approached them.

"State your name and business," demanded the one on the left, a surly-looking man with a thick, bushy unkempt beard and the eyebrows to match.

He pulled himself up to his full height and tried to put on a bravado that he didn't feel in the face of the two men who now held the key to his dreams.

"My name is Aron. I come from north of the mountain, and I'm here to see the Captain of the King's Knights."

The guards shared a look and laughed uproariously.

"Oh, you are, are you?" asked the second guard, a good bit shorter than the first with a stubbly unshaven face and the ruddy cheeks and nose of the town drunk in Aron's village. "And why would you be wanting to see the captain?"

"I have traveled over the mountain to become a King's Knight," he said, launching into a speech he'd been preparing in his head over the journey. "Goblins are threatening my home and…"

His pitch was cut off mid-sentence as the two men guffawed as though he'd just told the funniest joke they'd ever heard.

"Off with you, boy," said the short guard. "Go running back to your daddy's farm."

Then he turned to his taller companion and said, "A knight? That scrawny little girl?" They both laughed again.

Aron stood his ground, anger beginning to boil under the surface.

"The people north of the mountain need protectors," he said loudly. "The goblins have returned, and we need the King's Knights. I plan to…"

"Listen, boy," said the taller guard, cutting him off again. "King James don't give a rat's arse about the armpit of a village you live in. He's got bigger problems to deal with than goblins stealing chickens and pigs."

That broke something in Aron. All of the lectures that his father had given him on minding the livestock and taking his duties seriously, as much as he'd hated them at the time, now came rushing back to him. These two guards were telling him that his family, that the families of everyone in his village and all the other villages north of the mountain didn't matter at all.

"Those chickens and pigs keep a lot of families alive," he shouted. "I can help those families. I can be a knight, and I will, even if I have to go through you."

The short guard glanced at him, shocked, then a little wicked grin split his face.

"You're going to go through me, eh boy?"

"If I have to," Aron answered.

"What are you gonna do? Cut me with that pig sticker you got in your belt?"

"It will slice one pig's throat as well as another," Aron shot back with venom in his voice. Then the weight of what he'd said hit him. He regretted the words as soon as they were out of his mouth. He knew he'd made a huge mistake, potentially a deadly one.

The short guard's hand dropped to the hilt of his sword, and his face was fixed in a huge, hungry grin that promised violence and suffering.

"Aye, but most pigs don't slice back," the guard said.

The taller man put a hand on his companion's shoulder and whispered something to him that Aron couldn't make out, but the shorter man shook the hand off.

"Nah," he said loudly, staring into the boy's eyes. "The little rabbit wants a fight. I'll make rabbit stew out of him. Best run away now, little rabbit, before you get spitted."

Aron knew he should take the opportunity the man was giving him. He should turn and run away as fast as he could, run back over the mountain, go back to tending the sheep. He should admit that he'd been a fool and slink back home to his parents.

No. He wouldn't do that. This guard was no different than George, the bully he'd dealt with back in his village. If you didn't allow him to torment you, he had no power. Of course, he had to admit that George hadn't had armor and what seemed to be a three-foot long sword, but he had been a much bigger boy, and Aron had handled it. He was fairly confident the guard wouldn't use the sword on him. It wouldn't look good for one of the castle guards to kill a boy at the gate, would it?

Seeing the defiance in Aron's face, the short guard spread his arms wide. "Come and get me," he said.

Aron did just that. He dropped his pack, waterskin, and bow without thinking and charged. The guard calmly swung his fist, thumping the boy in the chest and sending him flying backwards to the ground. Aron sat on his butt in the road, a crowd gathering now to watch the confrontation. He took a moment to catch his breath, rubbing his sternum where the punch had caught him. It was going to leave a mark.

"Now, boy, get off," the guard said louder, playing to the crowd. "Go home and tend your pigs."

Hot tears of rage poured down Aron's face, and the guard's laugh at seeing them added tinder to the fire growing in his chest. He made a rash decision. He grabbed the knife that he'd stolen from the pig shed and spun, lunging at the guard. The man easily sidestepped the clumsy stab. He grabbed Aron's wrist and squeezed with crushing power until the knife fell from his hand. The man lowered his face close, his hot, stinking breath, causing the boy to squirm and try to turn away. There was no amusement there now, only anger. Then, he backhanded Aron across the jaw, his armored hand opening a gash in the boy's cheek and spinning him backwards. A heavy boot to the rear finished the job, sending Aron sprawling on his face in the dust. He spat out a mouthful of the red dirt of the road and rolled over, tears, mud, and blood mixing on his face. The short guard pulled his sword from the scabbard and started to stalk toward him, cursing with words that would cause his mother to wash out his mouth with lye if he used them, including a few words that he'd never heard before. His partner was pushing the guard back, trying to calm him.

"It's not worth it, Jarl," the taller man said. "You've made your point."

Finally, he turned and walked disgustedly back toward the gate, still cursing, while the other one turned back to Aron.

"Pick yourself up and get out of here you little scunner, or else I'll let him go. And if I see you around here again, I'll spit you myself."

He had no doubt the man meant it, too. This meeting couldn't have gone worse. Aron gathered his things quickly and scampered away, feeling the eye of everyone in the crowd watching him retreat like a coward. He knew there was nothing else he could do, though. He felt frustrated, afraid, and ashamed at the same time. Maybe what everyone had been telling him was true. He'd never be a knight, and after what he'd just done, he honestly didn't know if he deserved to be.

Seven

Aron retreated from the shadow of Lanfield's wall nursing his bruised ego and his wounded pride as much as his cut face and the abrasions that he knew would soon cover his body. His chest burned still from the guard's original punch, and his wrist ached where the man had clamped down on it. He'd been so sure of himself, so confident that the guards would at least allow him through to see the commander. He'd been naïve. Somewhere deep down, he'd known what everyone from his parents to the fruit vendor he'd just met in the city had told him was true. But he still believed, even now, that if he could get an audience with the commander, he could convince him.

His own actions in the face of being denied bothered him as well. When the guard shoved him away, he had reacted with primal rage. He'd grabbed a weapon, and he'd actually tried to stab another person. Never mind that he hadn't come close to touching the man. He'd tried, and that's what mattered. He'd never seen that side of himself, never thought he was capable of something like that. He didn't like this newfound darkness that lurked within him. Sure, he understood that he would be required to fight, and possibly even kill another person if he became a knight, but that would be in an honorable cause, right? Something worth fighting or killing over. Not because he felt insulted.

Aron cleaned the blood and grime off his face in a small stream he found just on the outskirts of the city. He looked down at his best set of clothes which he'd put on just before entering the city to make a good impression. So much for that. His mother would be horrified seeing his dress outfit covered in filth as it was right now. At least it didn't look like he'd ripped anything, which was a miracle given what had happened. He dropped to the ground, propping his back against a tree trying to decide what to do next. He knew there were other gates, other ways inside the walls. Maybe he'd have better luck from the southern approach. He wouldn't have the advantage of his nicer clothes, and he didn't think he could face another confrontation like the one he'd just had. The thought made him angry with himself. What kind of knight would he make if he was afraid of conflict?

With a sigh, he decided that he'd come this far, and he had to see it through, no matter how discouraged and embarrassed he was. He slowly pulled himself up and started marching back toward the streets of the city. This time, he took the narrower roads toward the east side of the wall instead of approaching the gate again. He didn't want to go anywhere near those two guards. He had believed the taller one when he said he'd spit him with his sword, and he knew he wouldn't be so lucky if they saw him again. He'd likely make it inside the walls if he did, but at best he would be sitting in a jail cell for attacking the city guard. He shook that thought away as he tried to navigate the maze of streets east of the wall. He wouldn't be so stupid again.

He'd walked for about twenty minutes, lost in his thoughts, when he suddenly snapped back to his surroundings. He'd wandered into a part of Lanfield that he hadn't seen in his previous visits. It was a seedy-looking area. Drinking establishments dotted the street he was on, and the sounds of raucous debauchery flowed out the doors and windows, even with the sun still high in the sky. Men and women hung out of doors and windows here and there along the street, beckoning to passers-by, offering them all manner of things that Aron knew weren't right. He tried not to stare or even meet their gazes. Instead, he focused on the red dirt of the road beneath his feet and picked up his pace. He needed to get out of this neighborhood as quickly as possible.

That would be easier said than done. A few more yards down the lane, and he felt the presence of someone on the street next to him, shadowing him. The boy fell in beside him. A few years older, he stood a head higher than Aron and outweighed him by at least fifty pounds. He recognized the type. Here was the village bully in the big city.

"Looks like we've got a lost little baby," the boy said in a whispered snarl. "What's the matter, widdle baby? Don't like the folks around here. Most of them will be really nice to you for a few coins. You've got some of those, right?"

Aron didn't answer or look at the boy. He picked up his pace again, until he was almost running. The bigger boy laughed and kept up with him stride for stride.

"Look, kid," he said. "We can do this the easy way or the hard way. The easy way is you just reach in your pockets and hand me whatever is in them. I know you've got money, and if you give it to me, I won't have to hurt you."

Aron continued to ignore the bully. He just wanted to get out of here. He glanced around the street, looking for someone that might help, a constable maybe or even just a concerned adult. There were no police in this part of town, though, and the few adults around who met his eyes just gave him grins that made him feel uncomfortable.

"OK, the hard way then," the older boy said, grabbing him roughly and shoving him into the shadows between two of the buildings that lined the road. One of the places was a saloon with music being played loudly by a group of minstrels and a noisy crowd that sang along. He knew the bully had chosen well. Even if there were a passerby willing to help, they'd never hear him if he tried to yell.

Aron was thrown to the ground for the second time today as the bigger boy dropped down on top of him, a meaty, filthy hand covering his mouth and nose. He kicked and thrashed to try to free himself, but it was no use. The bully outweighed him, and he knew what he was doing. He felt the boy's other hand reach into his pocket and find the few coins that were hidden there, all the money that Aron had in the world. He brought them up in front of his face to inspect them and snorted.

"Hardly worth the effort," he said. "Why didn't you just give them to me? We didn't have to do this. Now, I guess we'll have to see what's in that pack. Got to be something I can sell."

The boy rolled him over roughly and ripped the pack from his shoulders, then he plopped himself down on Aron's back, still pinning him to the ground as he rifled through the contents. Aron continued to thrash and try to throw the bully off him, but he might as well have been trying to lift the saloon they were hidden behind. He didn't even have the knife that he'd taken from the pig shed. There had been no way to try to recover it after the guard had taken it away.

He watched out of the corner of his eye as all his meager possessions were spilled onto the alley floor. He knew there wasn't much in there that would be worth anything to the boy, but those things were all that he had in the world. The bully had no regard for any of them.

"This is nice," he heard the bully say, holding up his small skinning knife. "I could use a good blade. I believe I'll take it. Maybe I should give it a try first, see how well it can gut something."

With that, the bigger boy jumped up, spun and kicked Aron hard in the ribs. His breath blasted out of his body before he could even react to the weight being lifted from his back. Aron rolled over, gasping and clutching his side in pain. He struggled to get to his feet, but the boy fell on him again. This time, he straddled Aron's chest and put his face so close that their noses almost touched. For the second time today, Aron's stomach turned at the smell of foul, reeking breath.

"Yeah, I think I'll try it out," the bully said. "Can't have you running out of here telling anyone as soon as I let you up."

He passed Aron's own skinning knife in front of his face slowly, taunting his prey. Aron squeezed his eyes shut and waited for the pain of the cut. There was nothing else he could do. He'd never felt so helpless in all his life. His quest would end here. He'd never become a knight.

"Now, just hold still."

"What's going on here?" The adult voice may have been the most beautiful thing that Aron had ever heard. "Hey now, boy, what are you doing there?"

The weight vanished from his chest, and he opened his eyes to see the older boy running full tilt down the alleyway that he'd dragged Aron into. He looked back toward the street, and a man was standing there looking down at him with a frown. He wore the seal of the King's Knights on the breast of his cloak, and Aron almost cried at the sight.

"Are you OK?" he asked.

Aron tried to speak but still hadn't quite regained his breath from the shot to his ribs. The knight, that's what he had to be even though he wasn't in armor, reached down to help him up. He winced as pain shot through his side. He hoped he didn't have broken ribs to go with the cuts and bruises that the guards had given him earlier. After a few moments, he was able to thank the man who had saved his life. Then he scrambled around picking up the things that were scattered in the dirt and shoving them back into the pack with the help of his savior. He held back the hot tears that burned his eyes, not wanting to show weakness in front of the knight. When he got to his bow, though, he did cry. The bow that his father had carved for him, that he'd been so proud of when he'd received it a couple of years ago, was splintered just above the grip, irreparable. It had probably broken when the bully had thrown him to the ground. Only one arrow had survived. He shoved it back into the quiver, along with the pieces of the others. Now he had no bow, no knife, no sword, and no money. He would be left with no choice but to go straight home—if he could even make it back there.

He stood with the help of the knight, who grabbed his chin and inspected his face. He suspected that it was full of ugly shades of purple and black at this point in addition to the cut. Even the knight's gentle touch sent shoots of pain through it, causing him to wince and jerk away.

"You need to take care of that, boy," he said. "That cut looks nasty."

"I can't," Aron responded. "I don't have any bandages or any money left. He took the last few coins that I had."

He gestured down the alleyway where the bully had run away.

The knight stared at him for a moment, sizing him up, then blew out a large breath.

"You'd best come with me, then," he said.

Aron didn't know where the man was going to take him. It could be to the same prison cell the guards would have thrown him in for all he knew. Still, he didn't argue. With his head hung low, utterly defeated, he followed the man through the dirty streets of Lanfield.

Aron meets Jasmine

"_Let's_ get you cleaned up and see how bad things really are."

The knight led him back the way he'd come, out of the seedy part of the city and its dangerous streets. The men and women who had accosted him on his previous trip through, though, remained quiet with the warrior by his side. No leers and menacing looks, no insults, as they passed.

They arrived back on the northern side of Lanfield, and the knight took him into the rows of homes and boarding houses. Finally, they came to a small, but well-kept cottage on a row of similar houses. The man turned and spoke to him for the first time since he'd told him to follow.

"You'll be safe here until you heal up," he said. "Then we can see about getting you home. It's obvious you don't belong here."

Though it was not the man's intention, his words stung Aron deeply.

"Is this your house?" Aron asked.

"No. I live inside the wall, as do most of the knights," he said. "This home belongs to the widow of a man that I served with. He died when his patrol was attacked, and rather than remain where she was reminded of him daily, she chose to move back outside the wall, where she grew up."

Aron took a moment to process what the man had just said, and something must have shown on his face. The knight stared down at him and nodded.

"Yes, lad, knights die in the line of duty. We're not immortal, and armor is not perfect. It happens much more often than I'd like.

"Now wait here. I'll need to talk to the lady before I introduce you."

The knight knocked on the door, and a woman that Aron judged to be just a bit younger than his own mother answered. She greeted the man with a bright and welcoming smile and invited him in. They talked quietly for a moment, and then he returned and ushered Aron inside. He introduced the woman as Jasmine.

She took one look at his battered and bloody state and made a sour face.

"Let's get you cleaned up and see how bad things really are," she said, pushing him gently toward a chair at the table and turning to shuffle around in a drawer for supplies.

As she did that, the knight announced that he had some errands to run, but he would return to speak with Aron once he was settled in and his wounds were seen to. Then he left.

The light through the window of the room that Jasmine had led Aron to was starting to turn the red of evening before the knight returned. She had cleaned up his face and announced the cut wasn't as serious as it had looked. He'd have a small scar, but it would heal. The bruising, she informed him, was much worse. She offered him a mirror, but he had declined to look at himself. He'd already seen the big purple blotch over his ribs where the bully had kicked him and the matching one in the center of his chest from the guard's punch. He currently had a poultice snugly wound around his body from waist to chest. He'd asked if she was a nurse, and Jasmine told him that she wasn't, but she had patched her husband's injuries often enough. He'd wanted to ask her more about the knight she had married, but the frown on her face when he'd opened his mouth had closed it again. She didn't think his ribs were broken but couldn't be sure. He'd just have to wait a few days and see if they felt better.

He sat, near drowsing, on the soft bed that stood against one wall of the room, exhausted from the ordeal of the last few days, when he heard a knock at the door. The knight stood there, quietly looking at him. Lost in his own thoughts, Aron didn't know how long the man had been watching him before he had knocked.

"You're looking better already," he said.

In his misery, Aron bit back a caustic reply about how much worse he felt. This man had saved his life. And he was a knight. A real knight.

"Thank you for helping me, sir," he said, and despite the bitterness he'd felt a moment ago, he meant it. "I'd probably be dead if not for you, mister…"

"Ah, I'm sorry that I didn't properly introduce myself," he replied. "My name is Devan."

"Mr. Devan."

"Not Mr. Devan, just Devan. Now, I'm curious what exactly you were doing in Sorrow's Reach?"

Aron looked at him quizzically.

"That's the name of the area you were in," he explained. "Bad place. Not somewhere a boy of your age belongs. How did you get there?"

"I wasn't looking for trouble," Aron said.

"You don't have to look for it in Sorrow's Reach," the knight responded. "It finds you, as you learned."

"I was trying to get to one of the gates to the inner city."

"You passed a perfectly good gate on your way."

"I…" Aron hesitated, but decided he'd better be honest. "I couldn't go back to that gate, not after what happened."

The knight leaned nonchalantly against the wall and motioned for him to go on.

"There was…an incident," Aron continued. "The guards wouldn't let me through. They made fun of me. I got angry. The one, I think Jarl was his name, probably would have killed me if the taller one hadn't stopped him."

A flash of anger passed over the man's face at that part of the story, but he smoothed his features quickly.

"And why did you need to get into the inner city?"

"I needed to talk to the Commander of the King's Knights, to tell him what's going on north of the mountain. The goblins are back. We need knights there to protect us, and…well, I wanted to be one of those knights."

Aron blushed, embarrassed. It had all spilled out before he could stop himself. It wasn't the planned speech he'd wanted to give, but there it was. He braced for the man's laughter, but it didn't come. Instead, Devan just smiled at him.

"Well, you certainly seem to have the spirit of a knight, I'll give you that. And you were ill-treated by the guardsmen. For that, I apologize. It's not the welcome we want people to have in Lanfield."

Aron hesitated, but couldn't hold the question in.

"You're a knight, right?"

Devan nodded.

"Could you get me in to see the commander? I know if I could talk to him, I could convince him to help and to train me."

"No," Devan answered, the word like another punch in the gut to Aron. "I don't believe that you could, unless you're from nobility or your father is a large landowner."

"We have a farm just over the mountain. Does that count?"

"I'm afraid not," Devan answered softly. "Even if your father owned your whole village, it probably wouldn't be enough to give you a chance of being trained for knighthood. I'm sorry."

"So, you're a noble?" Aron asked. Devan certainly looked nothing like the picture of a noble that he had in his head.

"Oh, no, far from it," Devan said with a chuckle. "My father was a knight, as was my grandfather and my great-grandfather. In fact, I can trace my lineage back to the beginning of the King's Knights, before things became political. Back then, perhaps, you might have been able to convince the captain, but that was a very long time ago."

Aron shook his head and sighed. "I know I could do it," he said.

"That I don't doubt."

"There has to be some other way in," Aron said, stubbornly. He refused to give up on his dream.

"Well, there are a few instances of someone being

accepted into knighthood because of heroic actions, but that hasn't happened in a long time. With the state of things today, I doubt that it would even still be possible.

"King James isn't a bad sort, but he's young. He doesn't have the wisdom or experience of his father, and he's mostly lived in peaceful times. He has the wrong people around him, and doesn't truly understand the importance of the King's Knights. I fear we'll pay for that one day."

Devan caught himself thinking out loud. His lips pursed and he looked to be a little angry at himself for the slip. Then he changed the subject.

"Enough boring talk of politics, though. Tell me a little about yourself."

"There's not much to tell," Aron said. "I came over the mountain hoping to be a knight. When I got here, I found out that everyone back home had been telling me the truth. I'll never be a knight. Then I got beat up a couple of times, had most of my belongings stolen or broken, and now I'm here."

The knight laughed at that.

"What about your parents? Do they know where you are?"

"No," Aron answered before thinking and regretted it immediately. He eyed the knight suspiciously, thinking perhaps he'd been trapped. This is it, he thought. Now he'll find out where I'm from and pack me off home to the farm.

"Don't worry, lad. If you don't want to go home, I won't force you, though I can't say what kind of future you'll find in Lanfield. Not much call for farmers in the city.

"I do hope, though, that you'll at least consider writing to let them know that you are OK. I know if it were my son missing, I'd be worried sick. If you want to do that, I'll see that your letter gets delivered."

"I'll think about it."

The knight nodded, indicating that was the last he'd speak of it.

"Jasmine needs some help around the house, and she says that, once you're well, as long as you carry your weight and don't cause any trouble, you're welcome to stay with her."

"Thank you," Aron said.

"Now, get some rest. We'll talk again."

Devan smiled and left the room, closing the door behind him. Aron watched him go, and wondered at the direction his life had turned in only a few days. Things were not well, but the thought that he was now friends with a real-life knight cheered him slightly. Despite all that he'd learned over his journey, he couldn't stop himself from thinking that maybe, just maybe, there was still a chance.

Nine

Several days passed before he saw Devan again. Aron's injuries were on the mend, and he had started to do small chores around the house to help Jasmine, though nothing too heavy or strenuous yet. His movements were slow, and his side still ached, but the pain was a little less each day. He was thankful he hadn't broken a rib. He'd also finally taken a look at his face in the mirror. It was as ugly as he'd imagined, though Jasmine assured him it would heal just fine, and aside from a small scar from the cut, no one would be able to tell the difference.

He sat on the lawn, pulling weeds from a little flower garden in the back of the cottage when Devan came around the corner. To Aron's surprise and delight, the knight carried two wooden swords tucked beneath his arm.

"You're looking better," he said as the boy stood to greet him.

"Feeling better, too," Aron answered, anxiously eyeing what the man held.

Devan looked down at the swords, as if only just noticing them, and smiled at Aron.

"I thought you might like these," he said. "If you're going to go around getting into fights, you might as well learn how to do it properly. If you feel up to it, I could show you a few things."

Aron nodded eagerly and took the wooden blade that the knight offered him. Devan spent the next hour teaching him the basics. Once he'd mastered the proper way to hold the sword, they worked on a few fighting stances and some very basic lunges and parries. Even though it was all very rudimentary, Aron was surprised by how difficult some of the moves seemed. When they finished, Aron's injuries had caught up with him. He was exhausted and sore despite the light regimen, but he was eager to continue and told the knight so.

"No, I love your spirit, but I believe that's enough for the day," Devan told him with a wide smile. "I'll come by again tomorrow afternoon, and we can work some more. I've got to be off now anyway. Business to deal with. Tell Jasmine that I said hello, and I'm sorry that I didn't get a chance to visit with her."

As he headed out the gate, Aron made a decision.

"Wait just a second," he said. "I've got something for you, too."

The knight looked surprised but paused to wait while Aron ran into the house and to the small room that Jasmine had given him. He emerged with an envelope in his grasp, a letter to his family that he had written two days ago and had been debating whether or not he would send. After a moment's hesitation, he handed it to Devan and was rewarded with a look of approval.

"Will you make sure it gets to my parents? Over the mountain, first farm at the bottom."

"I will," the knight answered. "I'm glad you decided to take my advice. I think it's the right thing to do."

"You won't tell them where I am, though, will you?"

"Don't worry. If you didn't tell them where you are, neither will the man that delivers the message. You can tell them more when you're ready. I think they'll be satisfied to know that you're safe."

He tucked the letter in a pouch on his belt, gave Aron a quick salute, and he was off.

The next couple of weeks passed pleasantly. He found that he enjoyed living with Jasmine. The chores he was given were light work for the most part, definitely not as onerous or difficult as the ones he'd had on the farm. Even with his least favorite—mopping the floors—he didn't have to worry about a cranky boar hog coming after him. Jasmine proved to be an excellent cook, almost as good as his mother, and of course, there were the training sessions with Devan at least every other afternoon.

Aron's bruising had mostly faded to light yellows and browns, and the pain in his side had disappeared. As often as the knight could make time to visit him, they clacked the wooden swords together in the yard for an hour or so. He had already learned a great deal in those sessions and realized how clumsy and awkward he'd been in the sweeping swings of the butcher knife he'd practiced with on his own. There was much more to handling a sword than hacking and stabbing. He enjoyed the sessions with Devan, but his experience at the gate, and his reaction to it, was still gnawing at him. He'd come to trust the knight through their sessions, and he finally worked up the nerve to broach the subject.

"Can I ask you something?"

"Of course," Devan said. "Anything."

"It's about being a knight and being in a real fight," Aron said. "I've been thinking about the fight I had at the gate. When the guard kicked me, something happened. I don't know what it was, but something I'd never felt before took over. I grabbed my knife, and I…well, I wanted to kill him. I wasn't thinking straight, wasn't thinking at all, really. He embarrassed me, and all I wanted right then was to gut him with that knife." Aron looked down at his feet. "I don't think that's very knight-like."

"Indeed, it's not," Devan said. He looked thoughtful for a second before continuing. "But I also don't think it's unusual, especially for someone who has not been trained. You gave in to a base instinct in the moment. Fight or flight. It's a trait that can be useful for a warrior, but you must remain in control, not get angry and lash out. Knights go through many years of training to build up their discipline and learn how to remain calm in such situations.

"It's not something I can teach you in these short sessions, but the fact that you know it was wrong, and it bothers you, I believe says a great deal about your character. I think you'll have a better grip on it if you face it again." Devan grasped Aron's shoulder firmly and met his eyes. "In the end, lad, no one was harmed, so it was a good learning experience. In a battle with a seasoned fighter, such rash action might cost you your life."

Aron nodded. The incident still troubled him, but he'd

trust the older knight's judgment that the moment of embarrassment would help him if need arose again. Devan had not steered him wrong so far.

"Have you thought more about what you want to do?" Devan asked, changing the subject. "Jasmine seems happy to have the help around the house, and still says you're welcome to stay as long as you want. But you realize, you can't stay forever."

From one thorny discussion to another. Of course, Aron had thought often of what he might do. He liked it here, but in reality, he knew it was a temporary solution. Eventually, he would have to either go back home or try to make his way in the world elsewhere. He still wanted with all his heart to be a knight, and the workouts with Devan had only strengthened that desire. The man had been very honest about what life in the service was like and the dangers it presented. It was certainly not all gleaming armor and glory. He talked often about politics as well, his face twisting into a sour expression as he did so, then he'd seem to catch himself and change the subject. That was something the boy had no desire to deal with at all. But still, Aron could imagine being nothing else but a knight.

"I guess there's still no way you could recommend me to the commander?" he asked.

"I could, and I would. But I'm afraid there's no chance you would be accepted," Devan answered honestly. "I wish it were otherwise."

It was the answer Aron had feared he would get, but it still hit him hard. Maybe he was just being a silly boy. Despite his desire and the happiness he'd found here, he'd been thinking more and more about home lately. He was surprised to find that he missed his younger brothers, and his mother and father. And maybe even the sheep and King Alfred.

"If I can't be a knight," he said after a few moments of silence. "Maybe it's time I thought about heading home. My parents and my brothers will be missing me, and I know my Da could use my help around the farm."

Devan gave him a genuine smile.

"I hoped that you would eventually come to that decision," he said. "Wait here a minute, I have a gift for you that Jasmine has been holding for just this occasion."

The knight went around to the front door of the house and disappeared inside. He emerged a moment later with a package, long and thin, wrapped in green cloth and tied up with string, which he presented to Aron.

He untied the strings. The wrapping cloth proved to be a new cloak, much better than the shabby old worn thing that he'd arrived in. Inside it were three items—a new bow with four arrows in a quiver, a new skinning knife, and the most important of all, a short sword. It was a plain blade with a simple wire-wrapped handle, but it was beautiful to the boy. He stared at everything there in awe. All of it was much nicer than the items that he'd come with, and it must have cost a small fortune. Aron knew he couldn't accept such a gift.

"I can't take these," he said. "You've done so much for me already. I don't deserve them."

"They're yours," Devan said. "I would consider it an insult if you didn't accept, and you don't want to insult a knight, do you?"

He gave Aron a warm smile at that.

"Besides, the knights' armory has plenty more just like

them for the noble brats that they will accept, and they won't miss these."

"You won't get in trouble for giving them to me, will you?"

"Not likely. Just consider it restitution for the way you were treated by the city guard when you arrived."

Ten

A week passed since he'd made the decision to return home, but he was reluctant to set the date with Devan. The knight had insisted on booking passage for him over the mountain in a coach. He would get there safe and sound in a single day. Despite the generosity, it wasn't the way that Aron wanted to travel. He had hoped to return the same way he came so that he'd have time to sort things out in his head and decide how he would approach his parents. Devan wouldn't hear of it.

He admitted that he was looking forward to seeing his little room and cot again. It wasn't nearly as comfortable as the soft feather mattress he was about to get into for the night, but in a strange way, he missed it.

He'd just pulled his shirt over his head to crawl into that comfy bed when a loud banging began on the front door of the cottage. He emerged from his room and shared a confused look with Jasmine. She motioned him back into the bedroom as she crossed to the door. He did as she asked but peeked around the corner to see what was going on. It was late, and no visitor should have been knocking, much less pounding the way this one was. Jasmine cracked the door a hair, leaving the chain fastened.

"Sorry to bother you, ma'am," said a gruff voice. "I'm looking for a boy. Country kid from the north, maybe twelve or thirteen years old. I've been told that I might find him here."

"And who is asking?" Jasmine asked.

"City watch, ma'am," the voice answered. "I'm afraid there's been a murder. We've found one of the gate guards stabbed in the western city, and we have witnesses, many of them, who saw the boy arguing with the fellow a few weeks ago. He threatened another member of the guard with the very knife that was used in the stabbing."

At that proclamation, another voice out in the street interrupted, and Aron recognized it immediately—the short gate guard, Jarl. The one who had wanted to hurt him.

"Killed him, he did," the man shouted, slurring his words. "'Arry embarrassed him the other day. I heard him say he'd kill him, and it was the pigsticker the little brat had that was sticking out of 'Arry's gut. He's a murderer."

"Quiet, you," the first guard said. "We'll get to the truth of it."

"Now, ma'am, if you'll just let us in, we'll get the boy safely up to the inner city where he can stand trial."

"Send someone for Sir Devan," Jasmine told the guard. "This house is under his protection. We'll sort it out when he gets here."

"Well, ma'am, I'm sorry, but we have a warrant for the boy. You can turn him over to us, or we're coming in to get him."

"She's protecting a murderer, she is!" yelled Jarl. "We should kick the door down and take them both!"

"Now you be quiet!" the first watchman yelled back at him. "If you hadn't been so sotted, maybe you could have helped him."

Then he turned his attention back to the door and Jasmine.

"I'm sorry, but emotions are running high on the watch, as you can imagine, what with one of their own being stabbed and all."

"Quite understandable," Jasmine responded. "But that's even more reason to wait for Sir Devan to get here and handle things in an orderly manner. From the sound of it, I'm not sure your companion out there is willing to wait for a trial."

"The boy's here!" Jarl yelled drunkenly. "She just said as much."

The guard at the door ignored him this time.

"I assure you, ma'am, he'll not get his hands on the boy. Now please just open the door. We could kick it down, like he said, but I don't want to cause any ugliness in such a nice neighborhood."

"You can go get Sir Devan," Jasmine said again, the iciness in her voice practically dropping the temperature in the room. "Or you can answer to him if you try to break my door down."

Aron had heard enough. He had a sick feeling in his gut that if those guards did decide to bust down the door and come in, he'd never see jail or a trial. Jarl wanted him dead, and if the others thought that he'd actually killed one of their own, he'd end up swinging from a tree somewhere in the nearby forest before daylight.

He threw his shirt back on and hastily crammed all his belongings into his pack except the fine new gifts from Devan. He threw the green cloak over his shoulders and belted on the sword. He swung the shutters on the window of the room open as slowly and quietly as he possibly could. He stuck his head out, taking a quick look to make sure they hadn't posted any guards around the back of the house. When no cry of alarm went up, he slid out the window, dragging the bow out behind him. He pulled the dark cloak around him and moved as slowly and carefully as he could across the yard and on to an adjacent street. As soon as he judged that he was far enough from Jasmine's home to not raise an alarm, he bolted into a dead run, legs pumping as fast as they would carry him, for the Mountain Road. It seemed he'd be going home a little sooner than he wanted or expected.

"Well, ma'am, I'm sorry, but we have a warrant for the boy. You can turn him over to us, or we're coming in to get him."

Eleven

Aron stumbled up the rocky path in the darkness, staying just off the main road in case the guards suspected where he had run and came looking for him. Only a sliver of moon showed in the sky tonight, offering no light at all to see where he was going. His foot slipped on a loose rock, and he found it sliding out from under him. The ground came up quickly to meet him as he fell on his face. He pushed himself up to his knees and examined his palms, now scraped up from where he'd caught himself. They were already burning. He knew he'd make better time on the road, but he'd also have less chance to escape.

As he stood, he paused long enough to look back on Lanfield, the place where his dreams had died. It was a much different view than the one he'd had when he'd left home. It had only been a few weeks, but it seemed like ages ago. Lights burned all over the city of Lanfield—torches, candles, oil lamps on streets and in windows. It was a much more impressive scene than his small village. He watched the city for a second. There seemed to be no out of the ordinary activity, no alarm raised in the streets at his escape. That almost disappointed him a little. Being a fugitive, at the least, would be exciting. Then he shook his head. What was he thinking? It would be best for him if no one bothered coming to look.

Aron felt a pang of guilt about leaving Jasmine to deal with the city watch. He had no doubt that she could hold her own with them, though. He also suspected that she would be fine. Devan would see to that when he got there. Aron was pretty sure that if he'd been caught, he wouldn't have been as lucky. Still, it bothered him. She had protected him. If she'd given him up, as she had every right to do, he might be dead now instead of on the run. And how had he repaid that loyalty? By running and leaving her on her own. That certainly wasn't very knight-like. But not many of the things he'd done recently had been, and he supposed, that dream was finished now.

But where, exactly, was he running? When he'd left Lanfield, he intended to head straight for home. But by the time he started climbing the mountain, he'd already discarded that idea. He'd foolishly announced to the two gate guards, and all the onlookers, where he'd come from. If they came looking for him, it wouldn't be hard to find him. Home, for the moment at least, was not an option. He couldn't go back to the city, so that only left him one alternative. He remembered the stories the trader had told, and as much as he didn't want it, his path lay on the road to the west, deeper into the mountains.

He wouldn't go far, he told himself. Just a bit off the main road. He'd find the first small cave or similar place where he could take shelter for a few days. That should be all it would take for this to blow over. He again felt ashamed for running as he thought about things. Jasmine would confirm that he'd been at her house all evening, so there's no way he could have killed the guard. Devan would sort things out and come looking for him. That's what knights did. It would all be over soon, and he could head home and forget about being a knight. It also gave him time to consider how he'd handle his homecoming.

Meals might present a problem. Obviously, there had been no time to throw any food into his pack, but he still had his snares, and he had the bow and hunting knife that Devan had gifted him. Higher in the mountains, there would be clean streams where he could fill up his canteen. It wouldn't be nearly as comfortable as Jasmine's house, or even his own home, but he could survive. He'd learned enough from his father to do that for a few days.

Mind made up, he braved the main road for the couple of miles he had left before the western path branched off. He moved quickly, ears open and glancing over his shoulder often. He dreaded the sight of torches coming his way or the sound of a horse's hoof on the stone road. Neither of those things happened, and soon, he was staring at the ill-used path that would lead into the unknown. He thought of the stories that he'd heard of monsters, dangerous people, and other horrors. He hoped they'd been exaggerated. At least, it wasn't likely that the Lanfield guard would come looking for him there. He hesitated for a moment, debating again whether to continue home or even whether to go back to the city and try to find Devan. He dismissed both and set himself on the western path.

He didn't bother to try to hide here. The footing on this road was little better than the rough country where he'd fallen. He'd hate to think what it looked like off the path. It was rarely traveled but had seen enough traffic that there had to be some sort of civilization down it somewhere. He just hoped he didn't come across one of those giant cats, or stumble into a colony of cannibals on the way.

After about an hour of walking, he came to a rickety old rope bridge over a gorge. He peered cautiously over the edge, and into the darkness. There didn't seem to be a bottom to it. He tried to tamp down the panic that leaped up in him. There was no need for that. As dark as it was, the bottom could be only a few feet down. Looking around on the ground, he found a large rock and threw it toward the center of the gorge, waiting to hear some sort of impact. It took several seconds before he heard a faint splash. OK. More than five or six feet then, and definitely farther than he wanted to fall.

He grasped the hand rope of the bridge and gave it a wary test. The whole bridge shook and clacked. The sound reminded him of the marionette show he'd seen at the village festival last spring. The puppets had been grotesque and had given him the same uneasy feeling as the path ahead. He imagined broken or missing boards somewhere out in the middle. He didn't want to brave it in the dark, so he searched the area for any place where he could shelter until daylight. He found nothing—not even a cranny or corner that he could cram himself into, and he couldn't remember seeing anything promising since he'd left the Mountain Road either. It was either cross the bridge or spend the rest of the night out in the open, with gods knew what lurking.

Aron stepped gingerly out onto the bridge, testing the planks with a foot. They seemed solid enough, if a bit creaky. He put his whole weight on the first board, and the ropes pulled taut. The bridge wobbled a little but it appeared it would hold his weight. It couldn't be more than twenty-five or thirty feet long. He could do this. He moved along slowly, holding the ropes to either side in a white-knuckle death grip as it wobbled and swayed beneath him. It was worst in the middle, and he feared it might turn and dump him into the gorge below, but as it began to slope back up to the other side, the shakiness eased a little.

It only took a few minutes for him to cross the bridge, but he felt like he'd been creeping along it half the night. When he stepped onto the solid rock on the other side, he almost collapsed with relief. He plopped down against a rock, breathing heavily, and trying to catch his breath, which he'd held most of the way across. He was still shak-ing, even though he'd made it to the other side and knew he was safe. Or so he thought.

As he rested against the rock, he heard a wicked little snicker behind him that warned him he wasn't alone. He snapped his head in the direction of the sound and found himself staring at a creature that was about his height, but more stoutly built. It stood at the foot of the bridge he'd just crossed. He couldn't make out many details in the darkness, but he could tell by the long, pointed ears and general wrongness of the shape that it wasn't human. Its shoulders appeared too wide for its body, and its long arms hung nearly to its knobby knees. It was dressed in animal skins that clearly hadn't been properly cured, and the stench of the creature made Aron scrunch his nose up even at this distance. Though he'd only heard stories of them and never actually seen one, he knew the thing had to be a goblin.

That little laugh, almost a gleeful giggle, sounded again

as the creature pulled a wicked-looking curved knife from its belt. With a quick, smooth motion, it turned and sliced the ropes holding the bridge. Aron watched in horror as it fell away, and he heard the smack as it struck the stone wall at the other side of the gorge. He was trapped. There would be no going back that way now. He barely had time to consider how his situation had worsened, though, as the creature began to advance on him.

Aron thought about running, but he'd have to turn his back on the monster to do it. If the goblin was faster than him, which it probably was, he wouldn't get far. He fumbled to pull the short sword from his belt, and he hoped that Devan had taught him enough as the creature charged. As it closed on him, he saw its wide mouth split into a grin filled with wickedly sharp teeth. A set of cold, yellow eyes locked into his, and in them, he saw only one purpose—to put its knife through Aron anywhere it could, and probably to keep doing it until he quit squirming.

As the creature came within range, Aron lashed out with the sword, but the monster easily batted it aside. It sneered at him then and lunged. He kept the blade in front of him, hoping to at least be able to block the goblin's strikes, and he retreated as fast as he could from the determined attacker. The curved knife swung viciously toward his throat, and Aron threw himself backwards away from it. Then, the worst happened. The goblin lunged for him again, and when he tried to get away he tripped over a rock in the path. Aron fell hard, his shoulders smacking the stone of the trail and sending the breath exploding out of his lungs.

The monster's momentum kept it moving forward, and Aron's legs got tangled up with the creature's feet. It went down just as hard as he had, but instead of its shoulder, the monster whacked its head on the rock Aron had tripped over. To his astonishment, it bounced back to its feet immediately, trying to get its bearings. It swayed now, though, and its legs seemed wobbly beneath it. Aron felt a familiar rage well up within him. He was reminded of his fight with Jarl at the gate, and he wanted to lash out without thought. He also remembered the lesson of that encounter and the lessons that Devan had taught him. He fought down the urge to charge in wildly.

Aron gripped his sword firmly as the creature stumbled toward him, and then he had his opening. When the goblin raised the blade shakily to strike at him, Aron surged to his feet, driving the point of his sword straight into the creature's chest. The beast went over backward, squealing like one of the pigs on the farm and thrashing left and right. Aron came down on top of him, driving the blade deeper. The monster pawed at the boy, trying to throw him. Claws came for his face, and Aron acted instinctively, releasing the sword to cover his eyes with his arms. He realized his mistake instantly, with his blade now stuck in the creature, and no way to protect himself. He glanced around for something he could use, but it was unnecessary. As the goblin tried to rise, the last rattle of breath coughed out of its mouth, then it went still and fell sideways. Aron was immediately and violently sick right next to it. It wasn't a dragon, but he'd slain his first monster.

Twelve

Aron woke stiff and cold. He didn't remember falling asleep and couldn't believe that he had. The last thing he remembered was the fight with…whatever that thing was. He had been sick and scared afterward. Then it was morning, and he was waking up with his back against the hard boulder that he'd hunkered against watching for more of the monsters he feared would surely follow.

He'd been exhausted even before the attack, but determined not to fall asleep with more of those things potentially out there. Apparently, his body needed rest and had other ideas. He figured he was lucky to wake up at all. If there'd been another monster in the night…he shivered as much from that thought as the cool morning breeze.

Aron gathered himself and stood, smacking his lips, trying to get the leftover nasty taste out of his mouth. First order of business, he needed to find a stream to refill his canteen and have a long drink. He wandered back over to the body of the creature he'd somehow managed to kill last night. He stood over the ugly thing and was almost sick again.

In the light of day, he confirmed what he'd thought just before the fight. This creature had to be a goblin. It fit all the nightmarish descriptions he'd heard of the monsters. Its skin was a mottled yellow and green. Its teeth came to fine, triangular-shaped points, almost as though they had been filed. For all he knew, they had. The nose was bulbous and misshapen, and the wicked yellow eyes he remembered looking into last night now stared blindly at the sky, a dull brown. The long, pointed ears held several roughly made wire hoop earrings. None of them looked to be made of anything of value—certainly not gold or silver. The monster smelled absolutely repugnant. He'd noticed its repulsive stench during the fight last night, but he hadn't had time to truly appreciate how awful it was at the time. He'd been too busy just trying to survive.

Aron picked up his sword, which to his chagrin was still laying on the ground next to the goblin. He should have had the presence of mind last night to try to clean it up and keep it with him in case of another attack. Yet another example of why he most likely wasn't cut out to be a knight. He tried to wipe off the green gunk that was the monster's blood on the rags it wore, but the blood had already dried on. He would need water not only to drink, but to clean up his weapon. Wrinkling his nose in disgust, he slid the blade back into its scabbard on his belt.

He grabbed his pack and turned to the west to head off in search of water and shelter— there was no going back the way he came—when he had a thought. Holding his breath and fighting off revulsion, he carefully opened the pouch at the goblin's waist. He shouldn't have bothered. It held only a few small bones that he couldn't identify and an old, tarnished coin of a variety that Aron had never seen. He felt something soft at the bottom of the pouch and pulled out a small rag doll. He flung the toy away in disgust, wiping his hands on his pants. He didn't want to think about how a child's toy might have come to be in the monster's possession.

He shouldered his pack and bow and headed off in search of a stream to fill his waterskin and clean his sword. He proceeded with much more caution than he had the day before. He didn't know a lot about goblins, but he did know that where there was one there were usually more—or even worse things. Dumb luck had saved his life last night, and he didn't want to trust to that again. He would be vigilant and avoid fights if he could. The battle with the beast had taught him that while Devan's training had given him some basic fighting skills, he was far from a master of the art.

He marched for an hour, keeping his head on a swivel, trying to look in every direction at once until finally, he found what he was looking for. A small, clear stream trickled down from higher in the mountains, cutting a tiny canyon across the trail he was on. He filled his canteen from the cool running water, then brought a handful to his mouth. He swished several sips around and spat it out in an attempt to get the remnants of last night's experience off his tongue. Then, he drank his fill. The water tasted better than any he'd ever had—cold, crisp, and refreshing. He instantly felt much better.

His thirst slaked, he set about the task of cleaning the gore from his blade as best he could. He had no cloth, but he did have his old cloak. He wouldn't need that anymore, so he cut a piece of it off with the skinning knife. He placed the sword in the water, downstream of the road, and wiped the gunk away as best he could. He grimaced as he did, not wanting to touch the stuff, but not having any choice. The last thing he wanted was to allow the fine sword that Devan had given him to rust. He dried it on the rest of the old cloak and put it away again.

The next order of business, he thought, was to find somewhere that he could take shelter. The wrecked bridge changed his plans, making it less likely that Devan or anyone else who came to look for him would find him. His stomach told him that was less important right now than food. It rumbled loudly, reminding him that he hadn't eaten for many hours. He scanned the area around the stream and to the side of the winding road. It didn't look promising. There was some scrub brush here and there that might yield a rabbit to one of his snares, but little else within close proximity to the road. He didn't want to wander too far away from it. Getting lost in this unfamiliar territory would be disastrous. The stream itself was not large or deep enough to hold fish here, not that he had any fishing gear. He was going to need a lot of luck.

He hopped over the stream, again looking for somewhere to set up camp nearby. It would be nice to have a source of clean water within walking distance. To his surprise, he found exactly what he was looking for only a short way beyond the stream. A cave mouth yawned in the side of the mountain. His joy was short-lived, though, as he considered the goblin from the night before. Could it have possibly come from this cave? Could there be more in there? If not goblins, what about bears or big cats?

He approached the entrance cautiously, peering into the darkness for any movement. He could see no evidence that it was being used. Tracks would be almost impossible to spot on the surface of the rock outside, but from what he could tell, it didn't look like anything was moving in and out. Aron walked into the cave slowly, using the deliberate heel-to-toe steps his father had taught him for stalking game in the woods around their farm. After each step, he paused to listen for any rustling in the cave or any sign that his movements had drawn attention. He continued in for twenty feet or so before the cave became almost completely black. The sunlight from outside barely reached where he was standing. He had still seen no sign that his would-be camp was inhabited.

Gathering together all the courage he had within, he called out half-heartedly.

"Hello?"

The sound bounced back to him. He waited for a minute, hand on the hilt of his sword, his mind playing out scenarios of animals or monsters rushing out of the darkness to attack him. Nothing happened.

"Is anyone here?" he asked, a little louder. "Anyone home?"

He listened carefully for any noise from the darkness—the rustling of animals or, he shuddered at the memory, the sound of that cruel little goblin laugh. But there was nothing. After a few more minutes, he began to relax a little. He had no way to explore the rest of the cave, but it would have to do. He would set up camp near the entrance, in the light, and he'd have to stay on his toes, alert to any movement or sound, especially after nightfall.

His temporary home secured, he set out snares in several of the clumps of nearby bushes and went about the process of gathering brush and sticks to help shelter him.

He piled small leafy branches around the entrance of the cave for camouflage and collected some smaller twigs and dried leaves in case he managed to catch a rabbit. His father had once tried to teach him how to make a fire with only a couple of sticks. He had not been very good at it, but he hoped he would have better luck today. Hunger gnawed at his gut, and his stomach was rumbling constantly as he stacked the brush up against the cave entrance to block the wind and hide his camp as much as possible.

Late in the afternoon, his shelter prepared as well as he could, Aron set out to check his snares. No luck. All of them were empty. He was afraid he would be looking at another long, cold, hungry night.

On his way back to the cave, he was startled by a movement in the brush to his left. His hand went immediately to the hilt of his sword, adrenaline pumping as he feared another goblin attack. Instead, he followed the rustle to a rabbit nibbling on the bush. Carefully, he brought his bow around and nocked an arrow. Not carefully enough. The rabbit must have caught the movement because it bolted, scurrying across the path in front of him. He followed it, but it was moving too fast. Then, on the other side of the path, it paused for just a split second. That was a split second too long. He released the arrow, and it speared the animal. He'd have food tonight after all. Aron smiled as he collected his arrow and, hopefully, his supper. Maybe things weren't that bad after all.

Thirteen

Aron skinned the rabbit in the last of the day's fading light, making sure to do it as far away from the cave as possible. If the remains drew predators in the night, he wanted to be sure they were not right on top of him.

He'd picked up a couple of forked sticks and a straight one that would make a nice spit. After washing the carcass in the stream, he brought it back to the cave, pushed the stick through the rabbit's body and set it aside while he prepared to attempt to build a fire. That was the only flaw in his plan. After leaving home without the means to make a fire, he'd sworn that he wouldn't make that mistake again. But, of course, he'd had to flee Jasmine's home so quickly that he'd had no time to even think about it.

The best he'd been able to accomplish when his father was trying to teach him was making the two sticks slightly warm to the touch. There was a very real possibility that he'd have the same results tonight, and even as hungry as he was, the thought of eating the meat raw made him queasy. That would be worse than being hungry.

He squatted beside the pile of leaves and twigs that he'd set up, picked two likely-looking sticks and went to work. He ground the sticks together vigorously for a good 15 minutes and was beginning to realize the futility of the effort. His hands and wrists were getting tired and sore. He touched a finger to the portion of the sticks he was rubbing, and it was hot, but nowhere near hot enough to start a fire. He picked up the pace and continued until his arms gave out, and he had to stop. The wood seemed a bit hotter than before, but there was still no sign of smoke or ember. Aron hurled the sticks across the dark cave and heard them clack loudly against the far wall as they struck. Forgetting himself in his frustration, he shouted a word that he'd once heard his father utter when a fox had gotten at their chickens. That word had later gotten him in serious trouble with his mother when he'd said it in the house, but no one was around to hear it tonight. At least, he hoped not, as he remembered his potential danger.

He slumped back against the cave wall, staring at the pile of sticks and the raw rabbit, his stomach growling. He was so close to dinner, yet so far away. He remembered what his father always taught him about never wasting an animal and felt ashamed. He had to try again. He'd rest for a bit and go find the sticks that he'd thrown. Exhaustion got the best of him, though, and his eyes began to droop as he sat there. Then, he was certain that he heard a voice. He bolted up, wide awake, looking in every direction. He peered into the darkness farther back in the cave trying to make out any sign of movement, but it was useless. He sat still and quiet, listening intently for any sort of shuffling or noise around him that might give away an enemy. The cave was quiet except for the gurgling of his stomach.

Then the voice spoke again, a deep rumbling bass.

"I could help you with that, if you'd like," it said.

Aron jumped to his feet, drawing his sword and looking around frantically for the speaker.

"Wh-who's there?" he asked into the gloom. "Who are you? Come out where I can see you."

"That, I'm afraid I cannot do," the voice answered. "At least not now. But the sound of your stomach is bothering me, and I'd say that rabbit would do us both some good. You could silence your stomach, and I'd no longer have to listen to it. Allow me to help."

Aron held the sword in front of his body, hands shaking, as he wondered what was out there and what awful thing was about to happen to him. Obviously, there was someone —or something—in the cave with him that didn't want to be seen. If it meant him well, why was it hiding? His mind played out all sorts of crazy ideas. Was it another goblin? Some mad hermit wizard who wanted to light the fire so that he could cook the boy who had wandered into his cave? He held his breath, searching the darkness for any sign of movement, ready to lash out at the first sign of attack.

The voice sighed.

"Do you want my help or not? I'd rather you take it and give us both some peace, but I don't want to impose on someone who is determined to solve a problem himself."

Aron remained silent, considering the offer. He knew there had to be some sort of trick, but what did he have to lose? He was already lost, cold, and hungry. If this strange visitor could give him fire, he could cook the rabbit and get a little food in his belly. At worst, he'd have a little light in the cave to possibly help him see whatever was there with him.

"Yes," he said finally, quickly adding, "please help, sir." It always paid to be polite.

"Very well," the voice said.

Then, it spoke again in a sinuous language that Aron had never heard before, and certainly didn't understand. It was a slithery sound that he couldn't imagine coming from a human tongue. The twigs and sticks he'd stacked suddenly blazed brightly. Aron stood for a moment, blinded by the light which stole his night vision. He listened again cautiously as his eyes adjusted, watching for any movement in the shadows. Still, he found nothing. All he saw was the flicker of the flames, and all he heard was the fire crackling. After a few minutes, he relented and sheathed his sword. Whatever he was dealing with could start a fire with a word. If it wanted him dead, he was pretty sure he never stood a chance.

He moved to the fire, placing his spit over it and setting the rabbit to sizzle. He carefully added a few more sticks to ensure his fire wouldn't dwindle. The smell of the cooking meat made him so hungry that he had to force himself to wait until he was sure it was fully done. He sat impatiently, turning the spit now and again to cook the rabbit more evenly. As the savory smell filled the cave, he longed to grab the stick off the fire and tear in, but his mother had often warned him about eating meat that hadn't been cooked long enough. Getting sick here would not be a good thing, whether his visitor was a friend or enemy.

Finally, he judged it was properly cooked, and he gingerly pulled a rear leg off the rabbit. The hot meat burned his fingers and tongue, but he couldn't help himself. His hunger was screaming at him. He pulled the rest of the rabbit off the flame and set it aside to cool while he savored the morsel he'd already torn into. By the time he finished, the rest of the rabbit was cool enough to eat. He shoveled pieces into his mouth greedily, being careful of the tiny bones. His mysterious benefactor was forgotten for the moment.

Later, as he sat staring into the fire, his stomach pleasantly full and drowsiness catching up with him, Aron's mind once again registered his possible danger. Obviously, there was magic involved in the way the fire had been lit. But if whoever—or whatever—was here meant him harm, why would he help? To fatten you up a little bit, said a cynical voice in his head. But he didn't think that was the case.

Whatever the reason, Aron had no way of finding out until the visitor decided to show himself. He may as well relax as much as he could. He'd sit here and rest his eyes a little. He wouldn't go to sleep, though. It was far too dangerous to go to…

As Aron's first light snores sounded, a deep chuckle filled the cave.

"Sleep well, young one. You are safe here. Nothing will bother you."

Fourteen

Aron startled awake. He must have dozed off for just a moment. It couldn't have been more than that because his fire still blazed high and didn't seem to have burned down at all. Somehow, though, he felt refreshed from his little nap. It bothered him that he had allowed himself to nod off not knowing what dangers lurked in the darkness, but nothing had happened, and the rest was worth it.

It seemed odd, now that he looked around, that there appeared to be more light in the cave than just a few minutes ago when he'd fallen asleep—a lot more than the fire would account for. He glanced toward the mouth of the cavern and saw the bright rays of the morning sun shining in. How was that possible? He couldn't have been asleep more than a few minutes, maybe an hour at most.

He stood, yawned, and stretched before walking over to the opening. He looked out, blinking his eyes against the brightness. It appeared that not only had he slept all night, but judging by the position of the sun, it was near mid-morning.

He stared at the fire, which was still crackling merrily, much as it had been the night before. It should have burned completely out hours ago, leaving only a pile of smoking ash, if that. There was certainly something strange going on here. Like dragons, he'd been told that magic was silly and didn't exist, but he could think of no other explanation for what had happened last night.

Aron stared into the dark recesses of the cave, looking again for any sign of his secretive visitor from the night before. He had been exhausted, stressed, and hungry. Maybe he had imagined the voice. Maybe his mind was playing tricks on him. Had there been someone in the cave with him who had started the fire by normal means and stoked it during the night? Had he actually gotten the fire going himself and tended it while half asleep? He might have been tired, but he was sure neither of those things had happened. He heard his father's voice in his head lecturing him about silly fantasies, but he couldn't deny what he'd seen and heard for himself. Surely, he'd stumbled into the lair of a wizard or maybe one of the shamans from the mountain tribes.

He pulled a long, burning stick out of the fire and waved it around, testing it. The flame danced, but didn't gutter and die down like a normal fire would. It blazed brightly, like the pitch-soaked torches in the village on a festival night. But there was no fuel. He'd gathered the branch himself, and it was just a simple stick. It shouldn't have been possible.

Aron fought his fear down. He was going to get to the bottom of this mystery. He drew his sword, and holding the flaming stick high in front to light his way, he moved cautiously toward the back of the cavern. The darkness parted in the light of his makeshift torch, revealing only the same rough stone walls and floor as the front of the cave. Toward the rear, stalactites hung from the ceiling of the cave, dripping occasionally onto a wet floor. About a hundred feet or so in, he arrived at what appeared to be a dead end. He stared unbelieving at the solid wall of rock before him. There was no sign that anyone else had been in the cavern. But that couldn't be.

Sheathing the sword, he ran his hand across the wall of the cave, slick with dampness. Surely there was some trick here. Maybe the wizard had cast an illusion to keep people out of his real home, but for a magical vision, it felt very cold and unyielding beneath his hands. He ran them up and down the wall, looking for some hidden secret that would let him pass and enter the rest of the cavern that he knew had to be there. But all he could feel was solid stone.

As he ran his hand downward on the wall, he struck a sharp rock sticking out just below waist height. The edge sliced into his palm, and he jerked the hand back with a hiss. When he did, the rock tumbled out of its place, striking the floor, the clatter echoing throughout the cave. As the noise faded, he heard a lower, grinding sound.

He spun at the noise, expecting some sort of trap. He held the torch in front of him, watching as a large square of the floor that he'd just walked across fell away in a whoosh of dust and musty air. What had been solid floor only moments ago now had a roughly cut square hole about four feet on each side. He crept to the edge of the opening and stuck his makeshift torch down into the hole. He couldn't see much, but he did see an ancient-looking rope hanging from just underneath the lip of the opening, knots tied in it at intervals. He leaned as far out as he dared, moving his flame back and forth, but could tell nothing about what might be at the bottom of the rope.

Aron considered things for a minute and made a decision. He carefully picked his way around the trap door and headed back to the fire to gather up his things. He grabbed his pack and bow and considered trying to collect a few more sticks to keep his torch going, but the one he was holding showed no signs at all of burning down or going out. The magical flame still blazed brightly at the end, so he decided to only take the one and hoped he wouldn't regret it.

Back at the hole, he took another look in, trying once more to make out any details of what awaited him. He knew what he was about to do was incredibly stupid, but his curiosity had the best of him. Surely if whatever was hiding down there had wished him harm, it would have come up and taken him while he slept. He wanted to meet the person—or thing—that belonged to that deep voice and thank him. There was also a chance, he thought, that he may find some help in getting home down there.

He sat his torch on the lip of the opening and grasped the rope with both hands, pulling on it. It didn't look great, but it seemed solid enough. Making up his mind, he dropped his torch down into the hole. He couldn't climb with it but would need it at the bottom. He hoped the magic would keep it alight, and his faith was rewarded. It landed about fifteen feet down, still lighting his way. He took a deep breath and swung his legs over the edge, grabbing the rope firmly and setting his feet on one of the knots.

The rope groaned and creaked, but it held his weight as he slowly and carefully climbed down.

He found himself in another cavern that was tighter and shorter than the one he'd spent the night in. It stretched off into darkness ahead of him. Behind him was another solid rock wall. A thorough search of that one for another trap door yielded no results.

Finally, he sighed deeply and turned back toward the dark hall. He tried to convince himself that his trembling hands were from the chill of the cave and not from fear. He wasn't very successful, but he still managed to get his feet moving in that direction.

Aron walked and walked and walked some more. No light but his magical flame penetrated the cavern, so it could have been hours or days that he wandered through the darkness. As he traveled the path, the cave sometimes widened so that five or six people might pass side-by-side. Sometimes, it narrowed to the point where he had to turn sideways to squeeze himself past. In one particular spot, he had to remove his pack and toss it through the crack ahead of him so he could shimmy through. No adult could possibly come this way, which made him wonder again what manner of creature lay at the end waiting for him.

He stopped occasionally to drink from his waterskin and take a brief rest. He managed to keep himself from falling asleep on those breaks for fear that he'd wake to find himself lost in total darkness with the magical flame burned out. Even after all this time, though, it didn't seem to have consumed any of the wood. The orange fire still danced on the very end of the stick without burning any of it away. It was hot like a real fire—hot enough to cook a rabbit, after all—and it gave off light, but it wasn't consuming the wood.

Aron remained baffled by that, but thankful for it all the same.

More than once, he considered turning back and trying to find his way out of the cave. In the oppressive gloom, it was easy to imagine that he might be lost forever beneath the mountain. The tunnel sloped ever downward and seemed to be delving deeper and deeper under the mountains. He thought he might eventually find himself in the mythical underground kingdom of the dwarves from a fairy tale his older brother used to tell him. Or, even worse, the underworld that the village priest often warned them about. Maybe this was some sort of elaborate trick of the devils that lived there to lure him down where they could capture and keep him there. He'd sat through a few sermons about people being led astray by beguiling demons.

After a while, Aron despaired that he may never see the sun again, but then he was given hope. He thought he saw just a pinprick of light somewhere up ahead. He placed the torch on the ground and took a few steps beyond it, giving his eyes time to adjust for a moment. Yes. He wasn't seeing things. He was sure that somewhere up ahead there was a possible way out of the tunnel. He almost broke into a run toward it but caught himself. He had to remember that what was waiting there might not be so friendly and welcome as the light looked at this moment.

He retrieved his torch and tried to fight down his excitement as he kept a steady pace. As he got closer, he could see that the passage opened, finally, into the sun. From a short distance, he saw dark evergreen trees and verdant grasses outside the mouth of the cave. He paused there and sat the magical torch down to consider the best way to move forward. As soon as it touched the ground, the flame sputtered and died. There was no going back now, not unless he wanted to brave complete darkness.

He slowly moved to the opening, trying to see any threat that lay beyond, but after so long in the dark, the light burned his eyes, so he used his hand to shield them. He paused just before the entrance to try to let his sight adjust. Tears streamed down his face as the sunlight pierced his eyes, and it took several minutes before he could fully open them and look at his surroundings.

The cave opened on a beautiful valley within the mountains. He recognized several different kinds of trees in the forest, and he could see a small, clear pool fed by a burbling stream just a bit below where he was standing. His eyes traced the stone walls upward, and they seemed to enclose the valley, rising sheer and high on all sides. He was amazed that such a place as this could exist. It shouldn't.

He stepped out of the mouth of the cave onto the lush grass there and turned to look back the way he had come. He allowed his gaze to travel up the mountain wall to a large ledge some thirty feet or so above where he'd just stood. There, on the ledge, was the most beautiful and most terrifying thing that Aron had ever seen in his young life.

Aron meets Dubloon

Fifteen

Aron staggered back, shielding his eyes from the glare. Sunlight glinted brightly off smooth golden scales as the creature sunned itself on the ledge just above the cavern. The beast was immense, even laying curled with its great wings folded against its back, it was taller than his family's home. Its long tail flicked lazily as it slept, curled like the orange tabby that lived in their barn to keep the mouse population down. A snake-like neck wrapped around the body, topped with a row of spikes that were a slightly darker shade of gold, as if they were tarnished. It ended in a massive head that looked like a cross between a lizard and an alligator except that it had wicked-looking, twisting horns extending backwards. He felt a strange mixture of exultation and fear. He'd been right. All the years his father had told him he was silly, he'd been right. He knew they existed, knew they had to exist. Right this moment, though, he wasn't so sure he was happy to be proven correct.

He wanted to run, even if it was back to the enveloping

darkness of the cave, but he couldn't make his legs work. He was frozen to the spot, unable to move, only able to stand and stare. He watched in horror as the dragon opened one appraising eye to look down on him. Then, slowly, it stretched out its sinuous neck, bringing its head down closer to where Aron stood. Large black eyes with slitted pupils that burned like flame stared at him curiously.

Welcome, my little friend, the dragon said, though strangely its mouth didn't move. It was as if he were hearing the voice inside his head. *I trust you had a good meal and a restful night?*

Aron recognized the voice immediately and wondered if, when he'd heard it in the cave above, it had also been in his head. Perhaps he just hadn't realized it because he wasn't looking at the creature. It was the voice of the benefactor who had lit the fire so he could have his meal. He'd imagined a wizard, but never in his wildest dreams this.

The dragon continued to stare at him, waiting for an answer. It tilted its head. Then the voice came again.

What is your name, youngling?

He wanted to answer but found that he couldn't utter a sound. Panic raced through his mind as he stared at this beast who had suddenly appeared out of his dreams and in the real world. Should he tell the dragon anything about himself? The creature had helped him last night, but could that have been part of some bigger plan? Aron chided himself for the thought—bigger plan for what? What did he have that the dragon could want or need? Still, he couldn't find his tongue.

Finally, the dragon nodded its head, as though remembering something. When it spoke again, it spoke aloud.

"Ah, you must forgive me," he said, the real voice

deeper and more gravelly than the one Aron heard in his head. "It has been many years since I last spoke with one of your kind. I forget that mental conversation often intimidates and confuses you at first. Perhaps it will help if I speak this way.

"Now, do you have a name?"

"It's A-aron, s-s-sir," the boy stammered, finally finding his voice.

"Very good," the creature said. "Welcome to my home, A-aron s-s-sir..."

"No, sir," Aron interrupted. "Sorry, sir, it's just Aron. I stumbled because I was nervous."

As soon as the line was out, he realized he had interrupted a dragon mid-sentence. He wondered briefly if the insult was enough for the beast to devour him on the spot. Instead, he chuckled.

"Very well, just Aron," he continued. "As I was saying, welcome to my home. I am called...well, I'm afraid humans are not physically capable of pronouncing my true name, so you may choose what you call me—as long as I approve, of course. I have been called different names by the few humans I've met over the years, and I have learned not to completely trust them. One of your kind once tried to name me Spot."

Aron thought the expression on the dragon's face as he said this might have been a smile, though he wasn't sure what a smile would look like on that mouth. In this instance, it terrified him, exposing the large, serrated teeth that filled the creature's maw. When he pulled back, the dragon looked at him quizzically, then nodded again in understanding.

"You have nothing to fear from my teeth, little one, or

my claws," it said. "So long as you mean me no harm, I mean you none.

"Now, little one…Aron, what will you call me?"

He thought on that for a minute. In all his fantasies, he had stood bravely against cruel, monstrous beasts that brought nothing but death and destruction. But that wasn't what faced him in this valley. Though still cautious, he was almost beginning to feel comfortable with the dragon. He'd never even imagined that they might have names or be able to speak.

He stared at the beautiful golden scales, shining in the afternoon sun, iridescent shadows playing over them as the dragon moved. A memory flitted across his mind from the market in Lanfield. Jasmine had sent him several times to pick up fruits, vegetables, and other small items while he'd been staying with her. He'd visited the fruit salesman he'd met his first day on a couple of those occasions. One day, a finely dressed lady had come from within the walls in search of a perfect fruit, which she thought she had discovered at his stall. She had offered the man a huge golden coin that glinted in the sun much like the dragon's scales. The merchant had protested because he could not provide change for it. He later told Aron that it alone would likely have purchased a large portion of his family farm. At the time, he thought the coin might be the most wondrous thing he'd ever seen, but certainly it paled in comparison to the creature before him. Still, it was the closest thing that he could think of. What had the salesman called the piece again? Ah, yes.

"Doubloon," Aron said. "I think I shall call you Doubloon."

He quickly realized how that pronouncement sounded,

as though he were giving a name to a pet rather than something that could eat him in one gulp.

"I-if that's OK with you, I mean," he stammered in apology.

The dragon tilted its head back and forth, saying the word several times in that deep, rough voice, as though tasting it and seeing whether or not it was to his liking.

"Doubloon," he said again. "Yes, I think that will do quite nicely."

Aron breathed a sigh of relief at his acceptance.

"But I forget my manners," Doubloon said. "You've had a long and difficult journey, and I am not being a good host. I suppose that you'd be hungry after your adventure in the caves."

He nodded eagerly. A long time had passed since he had eaten the rabbit, and he had traveled a great distance through the mountain—at least he thought so—to get here.

The dragon spoke another word in its strange sibilant language, and a sapling suddenly sprouted right in front of Aron. It grew at an amazing rate. In a matter of minutes, it had grown to full size, blossomed, shed those blossoms and was full of ripened red apples that would rival those of the fruit seller in the Lanfield market.

"You may snack on those while the rest of your meal is prepared. You humans still prefer to spoil your meats with fire, I suppose?"

It took Aron a moment to realize what his host was asking, then quickly agreed.

"Yes. We prefer our food cooked."

Doubloon sighed, seeming annoyed at the ruination of perfectly good meat.

"You like fish, I trust?"

Aron nodded again. He loved fish, but it was a rare treat. The armored fish that populated the river near his home were difficult to clean, and their meat was chewy and less than appetizing. Food fish came from far away and cost money his family rarely had.

The dragon sat on its haunches and spread its great wings. Then, with a mighty lunge, he leaped into the air, thrusting the wings backward as he did so. At the apex of his trajectory, he snapped them open again, and then he was soaring. He circled lazily a couple of times before landing next to the small lake across the valley. With a deft strike of his head, he plucked a large, silver fish out of the water, then leapt back into the air. When he returned to the ledge, he tossed it on the ground near Aron. At another word, a small fire appeared a few feet away from the boy.

"Tend the fish and cook it to your liking," Doubloon said. "I have no taste for burned meat. I'll hunt something fresh, so eat as much as you'd like. When you're done, you may bathe in the stream and change clothes if you have more. You're smelling up my home."

Aron, embarrassed at the blunt proclamation, sniffed at himself. He supposed he was a bit dirty, but he'd gotten most of the reek of the goblin off and didn't think he smelled that bad.

"My nose is much larger and more sensitive than yours," the dragon said with a chuckle. "After you bathe, sleep if you wish. You are safe here. Nothing will bother you. When I return, I should like to chat for a while."

With that, Doubloon once again launched himself into the air, the wind from his takeoff ruffling Aron's hair. He spiraled slowly up and up, out of the valley. Aron watched the graceful flight in awe until his host disappeared behind the peaks. He still couldn't believe that he had met a dragon, or how wrong he'd been about the creatures.

Once Doubloon was gone, he set about cleaning the fish and setting it over the fire. That done, he plucked one of the apples from the tree. They were delicious, with a crisp crunch. The juice practically gushed from it as he tore a chunk of it off with his teeth, and the flavor was unlike anything he'd ever tasted—sweet, tart, and perhaps a little spicy. He finished the first one and strolled to the stream to wash it down with a long drink of the cold mountain water. It, too, was clean, sweet, and delicious. After a few sips, he felt some of the exhaustion melt out of his body, as though perhaps the water had some magical revitalizing properties.

He picked another apple on his way back to the fire and munched on it as he lay back on the thick emerald grass and savored the smell of the fish cooking over the fire. He couldn't say why he trusted the dragon. He had to admit that it could still just be fattening him up for a meal later, but there was something in Doubloon's manner that put him at ease, even though he had several times been blunt to the point of rudeness. He supposed this could be part of the dragon's magic, and he could be under a spell, but at the moment he didn't care. He lay safe in a lovely valley, with plenty of food and the sun shining down on him. For now, that was enough.

Finishing the second apple, he turned his attention to the fish. He removed it from the flame and began flaking the flesh off the bone. He licked at his fingers where the hot meat burned them but paid it little attention. It was the best fish he'd ever eaten, better than even the finest ocean fish his mother had once or twice bought for special occasions. He finished it and took another long drink from the stream before bathing quickly as the dragon had instructed. He washed the clothes he'd had on and put on what had once been his finest. Jasmine had mended and cleaned them for him. He had to admit he felt much better afterward. He laid back in the grass, his hunger completely satisfied. Within seconds, he snored contentedly.

Sixteen

For the first time in several days, Aron didn't wake up cold or in fear. While he'd slept, someone had tucked a blanket around him, and he was quite toasty despite the chilly morning air. The grass and earth beneath him emanated warmth, whether from his body heat or some magical help, he could not say, but he wasn't going to question it. He could almost imagine that he was nestled back in the comfortable feather bed at Jasmine's home.

He woke and drifted back to sleep several times before he finally dragged himself out from under the blanket and walked to the stream to splash water on his face. The icy coldness woke him so completely that he wished he hadn't done it. He stretched himself, then wandered back over to the magical apple tree for a morning snack. He looked up on the ledge, and Doubloon was there, watching him with keen interest, as if trying to learn everything he could about his visitor.

Aron plucked the plumpest apple within his reach, though all of them looked perfect and delicious, and crunched into it before the dragon spoke.

"I trust you slept well."

"Better than in my own bed at home," Aron answered, and he meant it. He'd felt completely safe and cozy in the dragon's valley, despite the fact he knew he should be wary of the spellbound surroundings and his host.

"I brought you a venison haunch off my dinner last night for later," the dragon said. "It's in the stream now to keep it cool, but I will provide a fire when you're ready to spoil it."

Aron grinned at his new friend's aversion to cooked meat.

"Thank you," Aron answered earnestly, then he had a thought. "I should tell you, though, that I don't have any way to pay you for your kindness if that's what you're expecting."

The dragon snorted.

"Kindness that requires payment is no kindness at all," he said. "It's not often that I have company. That will be enough. It will be nice to chat with someone. I haven't had a visitor in nearly a hundred years."

"You're a hundred years old?" Aron gasped.

"Oh, about eight hundred actually, and I'm considered fairly young by my kind."

Aron let out a low whistle. Then the statement Doubloon had just made hit him.

"So, there are more dragons out there?"

"Of course. We mostly stay in remote places these days, away from humans. All they seem to be interested in is trying to stick something pointy into us to steal treasures from our hoards."

"It's true about dragon hoards, too?"

Doubloon raised his head, looking indignant.

"No self-respecting dragon would be without a hoard. But there is a difference between our collecting and the human yearning for riches. Dragons collect items that please us. Their value doesn't matter. Your adventurers might be quite surprised to see a real dragon hoard if they're expecting just silver, gold, and jewels."

Aron opened his mouth to speak again, but Doubloon held up a great claw, forestalling him.

"Now it is my turn to ask a question," he said. "What brings one so young as you into my mountains alone? It is a dangerous place for you to be."

He thought about holding back the true story, making something up that might please the dragon. But Doubloon had been so kind to him, and he felt comfortable in his presence, so he spoke honestly. He did leave out a few details that shamed him and made him look childish, but he told the whole story from start to finish, from the goblins threatening the Northern Reaches and possibly his own home, his trip over the mountain to attempt to become a knight, the murder that he had been blamed for, and his flight from Lanfield.

When he finished the dragon cocked an eye, studying him appraisingly.

"Tell me. Why did you want to be a knight?"

Aron began to talk excitedly. He'd wanted to give this speech to someone since the night he'd sneaked out of his home. He was desperate to convince someone, anyone, that he was worthy of the honor.

"I want to fight to protect my home," he said. "I want to slay goblins and…ummm."

"Yes?"

"Uhh…"

"It's OK. You can say it. I already know."

"Umm…dragons, I suppose," he whispered sheepishly.

Aron cowered away from Doubloon, then, expecting the beast to unleash a fury over the revelation. He expected anger and rage, maybe even to be obliterated by dragon fire. Instead, Doubloon sighed.

"You humans," he said, acid in his voice. "Ever since you learned to sharpen a stick, it's been the same thing. If you don't understand it, or it's not like you, it must be evil. It's why you fight so much amongst yourselves and with everything else."

He paused then, raising himself up to his full height.

"I'm right here, boy, and you have a sword. Why don't you come and slay me?"

"Well, uh, you're different…"

"Different, am I? Tell me, how many dragons have you met to judge me different? What did those dragons do to you that made you want to kill them so badly?"

Aron stood, staring at the ground, unable to look up into his host's eyes. He felt speechless and ashamed as he absorbed Doubloon's criticism. The truth was simple—he'd never imagined dragons to be like his new friend. He'd always thought them evil, unthinking monsters bent on killing and destruction. He'd never considered there might be dragons who would offer you a good meal and provide shelter and protection for you.

The silence stretched between them for several minutes. When the dragon spoke again, his voice was softer.

"Do not judge a thing by what you see or what you hear, but by what you know and experience. Indeed, there are dragons much like the ones in the stories you've heard. There are dragons in this world that I would battle to the death on sight. There are others whom I call friend who would do the same for other humans that I have done for you. Just like humans, each one is different. There are those like your gate guard, and those like this Jasmine and Devan. It pays to learn how to tell them apart, whether human or dragon."

Aron nodded at that. He'd certainly known his share of bad humans in his short life, as well as good ones. It stood to reason other thinking creatures would be the same.

"Now, since you're so eager to fight," Doubloon said. "Tell me, have you ever killed a thing?"

He had grown up hunting, and of course, on a farm, you learned very early about life and death and how the world worked.

"I've killed animals often for food," he said. "My Da always taught me there were only two reasons to kill—for food or to protect yourself and your family."

"A good philosophy. Your father sounds like a wise man. But that's not what I mean. We all kill to live. I mean, have you ever killed a thing in battle?"

Aron shuddered at the memory of only a few nights before. It seemed like a lifetime.

"A goblin," he said. "At least, I think it was a goblin. It was the first one I've ever seen. It surprised me, then it cut the bridge that I had crossed so I couldn't go back, and it attacked."

He described the monster in all the detail that he remembered, and Doubloon nodded

"That is, indeed, a goblin from the sound of it," he said. "Nasty things. They might be the exception to the rule about not judging creatures by what you've heard, though I still wonder sometimes if there might be goblins out there who are different. At any rate, I'm glad you didn't become his meal. You were very lucky to be able to defeat him with so little training."

Thinking back on the battle, Aron couldn't argue.

"It was an accident mostly," he said. "The goblin would have killed me, but our legs got tangled together when it charged me. He tripped, fell, and hit his head on a rock. He was shaky and confused when I…finished the fight."

"Nothing to be ashamed of," Doubloon assured him. "Your average wild goblin is a fierce fighter, not like those pitiful creatures threatening your villages."

"You've seen them?"

"Oh, yes. I've seen them massing on my flights. They are not true goblins. They have been tamed. Goblins don't hunt in packs unless there's something else driving them, like a human. Though they are certainly capable of raiding villages and stealing what they can on their own, I doubt the goblins are as much your people's enemy as the other humans behind the goblins. As I said, it's in the nature of humans to distrust and hate each other."

Aron remembered something then. He thought about the doll the goblin he'd fought had been carrying, and the story his mother had told of one of the recent raids in the Northern Reaches. Since Doubloon seemed to know much of goblins, he decided to ask.

"My mother said on one of the recent raids that they took a child. Do you think…" Aron trailed off, unable to finish the thought. The very idea sickened him.

"Oh, certainly goblins will eat a child," the dragon answered, and the boy shivered at the matter-of-fact way he relayed the information. "As I said, nasty creatures. But I suspect there's more to what's going on in your homeland than goblins looking for food and riches."

Seventeen

The days spent in Doubloon's valley were some of the best of his life, Aron thought. He lounged on the thick grass for hours and had long conversations with the dragon. The beast was curious about the most mundane of human things. He filled their days with questions about families and how they worked. He asked about simple tools. Most embarrassingly, he even wanted to know how humans relieved themselves.

Despite a few uncomfortable moments, Aron answered all his questions and then some. Doubloon proved an attentive listener and soaked up all the information the boy would give him. Just when he thought there was nothing left for the dragon to ask, he would come up with another question, always wanting more knowledge.

When not satisfying his host's curiosity, Aron tried his hand at fishing in the stream and the small lake that it fed in the valley. He'd always enjoyed trying to catch fish in the river back home, even though his father told him it was a waste of time since they weren't fit to eat. It was a different experience in Doubloon's domain. He had taken a supple limb from the apple tree for a pole, and at his request, Doubloon had retreated to his hoard and returned with a fine, but strong roll of thread and a few bone hooks he'd been able to dig up. He caught a wide and colorful variety of fish, most of which he'd never seen. More often than not, he provided his own meals, and all the different species here were quite tasty.

Doubloon still brought food back from his hunts, as well. The dragon always left the valley around sundown and usually returned with a leftover piece of meat from a deer or mountain sheep. He always took his own meals wherever he hunted. The first time Doubloon had brought a stag back and ripped into it in front of the boy, Aron had gotten sick, so he was now careful to spare him the sight. Occasionally, he came back with a slab of beef or domestic sheep. Aron always enjoyed the meals, but felt a little guilty, too. His father's lectures returned to him, and he tried hard not to think about who might have lost an animal from their herd and what it might cost them.

Doubloon shared just as much about dragonkind as Aron shared about humans. He had learned that the creatures were largely solitary, often going many years without seeing another of their kind. If need be, they could communicate over long distances through magical means, much like his host could speak directly into Aron's mind without saying the words aloud.

Over his time here, the boy had gotten more comfortable with that idea and sometimes spoke silently with the dragon. For his part, Doubloon seemed to enjoy having someone to talk normally with, and he would usually be the one to break the silent conversations with a spoken question.

Dragons, it seemed, were much more like people than he would have ever believed, yet quite different. The creatures apparently came in every color of the rainbow and very different configurations. A dragon in another part of the world might bear little resemblance to his friend. Doubloon shared stories of dragons across the ocean that were more like serpents and lived in the sea. He even dug a tapestry out of his hoard that showed a painting of one of those, which was odd indeed with its swirling whiskers and short, stubby legs. Doubloon spoke of dragons that lived on a remote island that had no wings with which to fly, nor any need of flight. There were dragons with six or eight legs like spiders and insects, dragons with no legs at all, dragons with multiple heads. All seemed to have their own personalities and ideas about the world.

The descriptions fascinated Aron, and he tried to imagine the creatures in his head as his host spoke of them. He wished that he might one day have a chance to see some of them in person.

He had asked Doubloon why there were so few dragons that no one believed they existed. Aron was astonished to learn that most dragons have only one hatchling in a lifetime, which often spanned thousands of years. A few lucky ones might have two.

"That's kind of sad," Aron said, thinking of his own three brothers. Even though they often annoyed him, he couldn't imagine life without them, and most dragons would never know what that was like.

"Not really," Doubloon answered. "It's a blessing if you ask me, given the behavior of humans—present company excepted, of course. If they believed we existed, we likely wouldn't for long. Young dragons, especially, would have trouble defending themselves. Better if we avoid contact completely."

"Do you have a hatchling?"

The dragon chuckled.

"No, no. I'm far too young for that, and it seems a lot of work for not much reward. Dragons spend five years providing for the mother while she nurses the egg, then once it hatches, she kicks you out."

"So, you don't get to know your families?"

"Not in the way of humans. We all know our dams. They raise us until we're ready to leave the nest. Some, but not all, know their sires. I knew mine before he died. If we want, we can find our dams or sires at any time. Mates, too, if we have one. I assume it would be the same for a sibling, but so few of us are blessed with them, that I couldn't say for sure. We have a certain sense of family, and if one member of the family is in danger, the others will respond if they can."

"Could we visit your dam then?"

Doubloon laughed at that.

"That's not a good idea," he said. "She's not a bad dragon, but she doesn't hold with humans. One tried to slay her for her hoard more than a thousand years ago, and she's never forgiven them. Dragons can hold a grudge for quite a long time."

Whenever one subject came up, Doubloon always rebuffed him and avoided answering questions about it: the dragon's hoard. He would only repeat what he'd shared on the first day they'd met—that they had one, and that it was not about the value of the treasures, but how much they pleased that particular individual. They often contained gold and gems because dragons, like crows, enjoyed shiny things, but most of the items may be of little value to others. He knew a sea dragon whose entire hoard consisted of pieces of something he called "coral" of all shades and colors. The description made it sound like rocks that grew under the sea. Having never seen the sea, he couldn't imagine such a thing.

Though Doubloon had occasionally retrieved something from his hoard to share with Aron or show him, he had been very careful to not let his guest know where it could be found. Aron had explored the entire valley in his time here and had found several caves. None seemed large enough for the dragon to squeeze through, and he didn't want to risk the trust of his new friend by looking. He'd once worked up the nerve to ask to see the Doubloon's hoard, and it had not gone well.

"I promise I won't take anything," he said. "I'd just like to see it."

"Absolutely not," Doubloon answered indignantly. "You are my friend, perhaps the dearest friend I've ever had, and I want to keep it that way. You are a good child. I trust you, and I think you believe what you say. But I have seen the greed of humans, and I won't allow it to take you."

Aron had not asked again. He was sure he could control himself in the presence of his friend's riches, but the dragon was convinced otherwise. He decided it was best not to speak of it. He enjoyed Doubloon's company, and he could tell by the beast's manner that if he continued to push, he might lose that. He could understand where the mistrust of humans had come from, but he hoped he could one day prove to Doubloon that some could be trusted. Like dragons, he knew they weren't all bad.

Eighteen

The weeks in the secluded valley had passed pleasantly with his dragon friend. Although Aron occasionally felt a twinge of regret and homesickness for his family, he didn't think he was prepared to face them again. He'd spent a lot of time thinking about his parents' disappointment in him and how he would approach the reunion. And for all he knew, he was still wanted as a murderer. Surely Devan would have straightened things out by now, but he couldn't know that without leaving the mountains. He wasn't quite ready to take that step yet. He knew it was selfish, but he enjoyed his life with Doubloon. He was safe, he had no responsibilities, and his conversations with the dragon were fascinating.

When Doubloon's shadow passed over him, much like he'd imagined in his daydreams back in the farm pasture, he broke from his thoughts of the outside world and stared up eagerly. Usually, the dragon was back from his hunts by the time the boy woke in the morning. He was loathe to fly during the daytime for fear of being spotted by humans.

Aron had been wondering what had delayed his friend today.

"I was worried that something might have happened to you," he said as the dragon landed on the grass in front of him.

Doubloon snorted.

"No need to worry about me," he said proudly. "I've been here longer than anything else in these mountains and nothing would dare impede me.

"I have been thinking, though, and I needed some time this morning to consider."

The dragon still seemed to be making up his mind about whatever it was as he looked down on Aron.

"A doubloon for your thoughts," the boy said with a laugh.

Doubloon looked at him quizzically, tilting his head. Aron waved the comment away.

"Sorry, bad joke. I'll explain later. But what have you been thinking about?"

"I've been considering whether or not to offer you a gift," he said. "It's something I've never given anyone before, a gift that I daresay few, if any, of your kind have ever received."

Aron's breath caught in his throat. Could this be the opportunity he'd been waiting for? Would he finally see an actual dragon hoard? Doubloon had been so adamant about keeping his treasures private, but he had asked the dragon for nothing else and could think of no other thing this gift might be.

"What did you have in mind?" he asked cautiously, heart pounding loudly in his chest.

"Would you like to fly?"

It took a moment for Aron to register what his friend had just said, and he stared dumbly at Doubloon. The dragon cocked his head questioningly, and Aron realized he was waiting for an answer. He nodded eagerly, still not quite able to find words. The gift wasn't the dragon hoard after all. It was something so much better. He had often imagined what it would be like to soar over the peaks as he'd so often watched his host do as he left in the evenings. He shook with both nervousness and excitement. The thought of soaring high above the earth scared him to death, but he really wanted to feel the wind rushing by him as he looked down on the world. He was speechless. Doubloon looked at him with concern.

"You're shaking," the dragon said. "Did I say something to upset you?"

"No, no, no." The words spilled out in a rush. "I just don't know what to say. I never dreamed…"

"I've never taken on a rider, but I suspect it will be tricky, especially at first. You must do exactly as I tell you. Whatever I say, you must do it immediately or else we may both go tumbling to the ground. Do you understand?"

"Yes," he responded, nodding his head rapidly. "You say it, I do it."

The dragon nodded back, then knelt in front of Aron, extending a wing to the ground.

"Climb my wing."

Aron scrambled up on to the dragon's back. He stepped off the wing onto scales that were glassy and slick, and he almost slid back to the ground.

"Careful," the dragon said.

This may be tougher than the boy had thought. He

slowly pulled himself up, slipping and sliding to get his legs straddling the beast's back.

"Place yourself just ahead of my wings and rest your legs where they connect with my body," the dragon said. "That should help you stabilize, and you can hold on to my mane for support."

Aron settled himself where instructed and reached out to grab one of those tarnished gold spines that extended down the dragon's neck from the back of his head to near where he sat. He had expected something hard and sharp from the look of them. Instead, the spike was soft, almost squishy in his hands. Aron gasped and rubbed his hand along the spine, feeling it. Then he gripped it tightly.

"That doesn't hurt, does it?"

"No chance of that, little one," he answered. "In this form, they are mostly for display, but they can also be used for defense if needed."

"How? They're so soft."

"Release it and sit back a little."

Aron did as he'd been instructed. Doubloon's neck muscles clinched suddenly, and Aron heard a pop. Bone-hard spikes shot up into the skin of the spines on his neck, stretching them out and turning them into sharp and deadly defenses.

"It's a nasty shock for any dragon that tries to grab me around the neck," Doubloon said. "And yes, we do occasionally have to fight one of our own."

Aron could imagine that the day wouldn't end well for the enemy. Then he tried to picture in his head what a dragon battle might look like. Now that would be something to see. Or maybe not, at least not if Doubloon were involved. He definitely didn't want his friend getting hurt.

Doubloon retracted his spikes and instructed the boy to hang on to his mane tightly. He did so and attempted to grip the dragon's sides with his knees as he would a horse, but the creature's body was much too large and slippery for that. Still, he did the best he could. The fear of sliding off and plummeting to the earth as they flew high in the sky almost overwhelmed Aron, but he was not about to turn back at this point. How many people in the world could say that they'd ever flown on the back of a dragon? He might even be the first.

"Hang on," Doubloon said, crouching and launching himself into the air. That was almost the end of their flight as Aron's legs slid up and off the dragon's body at the sudden movement. He only barely hung on to the soft spine of his friend's mane until they leveled off and began to rise slowly in a circle. Aron's body fell back onto the dragon's shoulders, and he worked his knees back around the beast's body as best he could.

"Sorry about that," Doubloon said. "As I said, I've never had a rider before, so I wasn't sure what would happen. Bend your knees, tuck your feet beneath my wings, and lean forward slightly. That might help you hang on."

Aron followed the instructions and found that he did feel much more stable in that position with more of his body in contact with the dragon. It limited his view a bit, but that hardly mattered. He was flying—really flying. He could feel the ebb and flow of muscle beneath him as Doubloon flapped his wings lazily, circling higher and higher above the valley.

The boy's eyes drifted down below them, and the result was almost disastrous. His head spun as he saw the ground far, far beneath them. They had soared higher and faster than he'd imagined. He could see the whole of the valley stretched out, the lake where he'd fished looking like nothing more than a mud puddle from this height. He clutched at Doubloon's mane fiercely.

"Easy," came the reassuring voice of the dragon. "Keep calm. I'll make no sudden movements on this flight, and we can return to the ground whenever you want. Should you fall, trust that I will catch you. All will be well."

Aron remained terrified, but he did feel somewhat reassured. Doubloon would catch him, and even if he couldn't, surely the dragon knew some spell that would stop or at least cushion his fall, right? He had been true to his word about everything else, and despite his instincts screaming that he was in imminent danger, Aron felt safe with his magical friend.

The first flight didn't last long, nor did they travel far. Doubloon flew in slow circles, and Aron never lost sight of their valley. In the distance he could just make out a large clump of buildings that must be Lanfield. He realized that perhaps he had not traveled as far from the city as he'd thought. Of course, it was tough to judge distance from the heights at which they soared. He could see for what must have been miles in every direction. He again wondered, briefly, if he were still wanted in the city, but the landscape below him quickly pulled his attention back from that line of thought. It didn't matter what was going on in the human world. He was flying on the back of a magnificent dragon. Nothing and no one could touch him here. For the moment, he was invincible.

Nineteen

Their flights ranged farther and farther over the days that followed. Doubloon seemed to enjoy Aron's delight just as much as the view from high above the world fascinated the boy. After a few mishaps, none thankfully that resulted in a mid-air rescue, the dragon and the boy had worked together to fashion a kind of harness to help him stay aboard. They'd made a few adjustments to the design until it worked flawlessly, giving Doubloon more freedom to fly without worrying about his passenger. The dragon could even spin upside down, and Aron was safe, though the boy had made it known that he was not eager to try that again after their one experiment.

Aron had gotten much more comfortable on the dragon's back and with the heights. He no longer had to cut them short from dizziness, and he'd overcome the airsickness that had left him in misery, stomach aching and churning, after the first few flights. Dragon and boy both looked forward to their daily trips into the air.

This morning's flight felt a little different, though Aron

couldn't say why. Doubloon had been unusually reserved before they had taken off. The boy exulted in the cool autumn breezes blowing over him as Doubloon circled slowly into the sky as usual. He rose higher and higher, above the mountain peaks around them, and then set off at a leisurely pace toward the north. In all their trips, they had never gone in this direction. It was as if his friend had purposely avoided it, and Aron knew why. He suspected where they were going, but he remained silent, not sure how he felt about their destination.

They'd only traveled a few minutes when he spotted a familiar sight. Though he'd never seen it quite like this, it was unmistakable to him. He looked down from the clouds on the line of buildings and fields where he had grown up. Somewhere down there, his father and brothers were tending the animals and the crops. His mother was likely cleaning up from breakfast and getting ready to prepare lunch. Aron felt both a pang of homesickness and more than a little trepidation as they soared ever closer to the loved ones that he'd left behind in the night. He sighed deeply.

"You recognize it, then," Doubloon said, as if sensing his unease. "We could fly closer and take a look if you want. Honestly, I'd like to see for myself the place I've heard so many stories about"

That struck Aron as very strange. In all their flights, the dragon had been adamant about avoiding any place at all inhabited by humans. He'd been hidden away in the mountains for many years, unknown to people, and he wanted things to remain that way. Aron had urged him several times to turn toward Lanfield, as he wanted to see the city from high above, but his friend had always flatly refused.

"You'd fly over my village in broad daylight?" he asked, confused.

Doubloon was quiet for a moment, and then he sighed. He continued his slow flight toward the boy's home, determined, but reluctant.

"I never told you what happened to my sire."

"No, you didn't."

"He was shot down by a human," Doubloon said flatly.

Aron gasped. His friend's distrust of humans in general made much more sense now. His dam had been attacked and his father killed by them. Knowing that, he was amazed that the dragon hadn't attacked him on sight, and it was even more unbelievable that Doubloon had actually helped him and befriended him.

"I'm sorry," Aron said, genuinely saddened by the revelation.

"He was too proud, considered himself invincible," the dragon continued. "Our scales will protect us from just about anything your kind can throw our way. The shot was either very lucky or very good. The arrow struck him in the eye. He fell to the ground, half-blinded and in pain, and the villagers descended on him with axes, farm implements, and anything else they had at hand.

"My dam told me the story when I was young to keep me away from humans, and all these years, I've believed that she was right. The few humans I've encountered throughout my life seemed to confirm my feelings about them. They always seemed friendly at first, but each and every one had ulterior motives. I've never met one who earned my trust—until now."

Aron gulped, feeling a lump in his throat and an ache in his heart. He didn't know what to say. He longed to make up for what his kind had done to Doubloon's relatives, but he knew there was no way that he could. Instead of speaking, he leaned further forward, gripping the dragon's neck in the closest thing to a hug that he could manage. Doubloon raised his neck to the boy and exhaled in contentment.

"Now, would you like to check in on your family?" he asked. "You've been gone a very long time, and I thought you might miss them. I will not fly too close. Family or not, I still do not trust the others. I will stay high in the clouds, but maybe you can get a look without us being seen."

Aron wanted nothing more. As they had come closer to the village, his homesickness had become more and more acute, winning out against the uncertainty that he also felt about his reception. He hadn't realized just how much he'd missed his parents and siblings until he looked again on the village. Now he could see the road winding down off the mountain to the southern end of town. Between his time in Lanfield and his time with Doubloon, it had been nearly two months since he'd set off up that path under the cover of night. He stared at the field where his father had scolded him, reliving that moment and reflecting on just how much he'd learned since that fateful day. He felt no sense of victory in the fact that he'd obviously proven his father wrong—about dragons, at least. Finally, he saw the roof of his house. They were close now, and Doubloon began to rise higher. Aron said nothing, understanding the dragon's reluctance, but still he hoped he'd at least be able to get a glimpse of his family.

He scanned the rooftops, trying to recognize all the buildings in the village, but they looked much different from far above than they did on the dirt paths between them. A few were recognizable from this angle, but most he had to figure out based on where they were in relation to the farm. Then, he glanced out beyond his home and something else caught his eye. Suddenly, his attention snapped away from warm but nervous thoughts of friends and family. Their reaction to his homecoming felt far less important than what he feared lay on the fields in the distance. His breath caught in his throat at the sight of a dark mass only miles from the village and moving fast toward it.

"Look, there," he said to Doubloon. "To the north. What is it?"

He hoped the dragon could give him a different answer than the one he knew to be true. He did not.

"We should go back," Doubloon said nervously.

"No. I need to see," Aron responded. "Take us there… please."

Doubloon blew out a reluctant sigh and began to rise even higher, taking them deeper into the clouds. It was cold up there and damp. Aron shivered and pulled his cloak tighter around him, but did not complain. He understood the need to remain hidden, not only from the people of his village but from what he feared they would find ahead.

They flew on until, finally, they were directly over the squirming black mass that he'd spotted from a distance. Aron leaned over Doubloon's neck, peering down through the passing openings in the clouds. Through the wisps of vapor, he saw thousands of tiny figures moving along the ground toward his village. He could tell little about them, though.

"Can we get a little closer?" he asked. "I can't see what's going on."

The dragon sighed again, then said a word in his

strange language. Aron felt dizzy and disoriented and closed his eyes tightly against the nausea that threatened to overtake him. When he opened them again, it was like he was soaring directly over the mass of creatures, even though he and Doubloon were still safely high up in the clouds. It felt very strange, but the novelty of it died quickly when he realized what he was seeing below.

Rank upon rank of them marched directly toward his village. Ugly, monstrous figures that looked exactly like the thing he'd killed in the mountains—misshapen creatures in shades of gray and green and yellow with pointy ears, warts, fangs, and clawed hands and feet. Goblins. Scattered among them, he could see a mix of human troops that seemed a little more organized. Just as Doubloon had said, they appeared to be driving the monsters, shouting at them, some brandishing whips or prods to keep the creatures together and moving in the right direction.

"You have to take me home," Aron said. "I have to warn them. Land me in the field south of town. I'll protect you; I promise. We have to let them know, give them time to get prepared."

"I'm afraid, little one, that you cannot protect me," the dragon answered. "I've seen how humans react to my kind, and they would not even pause to listen to you. I have no desire to fight your kin, so I will not show myself to them. But you are right. They should be warned. I will put you down as near to the village as I can without being seen. You have time. It will take the army at least a half day's march to reach you."

Doubloon took him back near the road south of the village before finding an area that was somewhat screened from the homes by trees where he could land and let the boy get off his back, he hoped without being seen. Likely, the attention of the villagers was already turned to the north, he thought, though he didn't want to tell the boy that. An army the size of the one marching on the village couldn't get that close without people knowing about it.

Aron leaped down from the dragon's back almost before they touched the ground, eager to bring the news of what was coming.

"You'll be here?"

"If not here, nearby," the dragon assured him. "When you return, I will see you."

Twenty

Aron dashed into his house and straight into a bustle of activity. His mother and brothers were hustling around their home packing things up. He burst into the middle of it, flustering them for a few moments. When she spotted him, his mother dropped the clothes that she was cramming into a sack and just stared at him for a moment, eyes wide in shock. When the realization of what she was seeing set in, she burst into tears and ran across the room to embrace him. She fell to her knees and sobbed over his shoulder as she hugged him so tightly that he could barely breathe. Her grip was uncomfortably snug, but at the same time one of the best things he'd ever felt. After a minute, she pushed him away and held him at arm's length. She looked at him long and hard, her green eyes now reddened from the droplets that were still streaming and tracing a path down her face. She gently traced the scar, left by Jarl's gauntlet, with her thumb. She frowned sharply at that.

"I thought we'd never see you again," she said, a hint of

anger warring with the concern in her voice. "We got your letter, but it didn't say much. What's happened to you? Where have you been? What have you been doing all this time?"

He felt the words bubbling up inside him, ready to pour out in a long story of his time in Lanfield and his flight into the mountains. He wanted to tell her that he'd been right. Dragons really did exist, and he'd met one. But he bit down on the desire to fill her in on his adventures as he remembered the reason he'd come—the army of darkness which was marching across the fields outside of town.

"Everywhere," he answered in a rush. "I've been everywhere, and I'll tell you all about it. But I need to know where Da is right now. It's important. I have to find him and warn him."

"He's at the north end of the village with the other men, but…"

Aron didn't give her a chance to finish the thought. He broke free and bolted out the door, hitting the main road to the northern edge of the village at a run. He was halfway there before he realized what his mother's words and the activity that he'd seen in the house had most likely meant—that they were already aware of the threat and preparing for it. His mother and his younger brothers had been packing up everything they could carry. That meant the men were preparing to fight, and the women and children to flee.

He kept going anyway. He was determined to be sure and to do what he could to defend the village. He found his father helping some of the other men and older boys lash together sharpened trunks of small trees to form a line of defensive spikes around the north end of the village. Belted around his waist, he wore the heavy sword that Aron had rarely seen outside of the trunk in his parents' bedroom. Aron's nerve started to fade as he approached; he feared this reunion more than anything else. He didn't know exactly how his father would greet him, but he expected it would not be nearly as warmly as his mother.

He briefly considered retreating home, back to the shelter of his mother's love, since the village was clearly already warned of the coming attack. He paused a moment, thinking over his options. Running away now would not be very knight-like, though. Before he could make his final decision, his father turned and stared at him for a moment, almost as if he didn't recognize him. Then the big man crossed the distance between them in only a few steps and lifted his son in a crushing hug. There were no tears in this reunion, and the embrace was brief, much shorter than his mother's, but it meant just as much to him, perhaps more. It was very unlike his father. The moment was fleeting, though, as his Da dumped him unceremoniously back to the ground. He took a step back, crossed his arms and fixed Aron with a cold glare that promised there would be repercussions for his actions in the near future.

"You have a lot to answer for, young man," he said. "And you will. But there's no time now. We've got trouble coming."

"I came to warn you about the goblins," Aron blurted out, not knowing what else to say.

"I'm not sure how you know about them, but how could we miss them?" He gestured to the north where clouds of dust were rising into the air, marking the position of the enemy forces.

Aron felt silly. Of course they would have seen them

coming. He stared at the ground, embarrassed and ashamed, unable to meet his father's eyes.

"I hear you've had quite the adventure," his father said. "But I hope you've gotten it out of your system now. It was a foolish thing all around, what you did. Commander Kyle told us all about it when he arrived, but he had no idea where you'd fled. He feared you were lost or dead. We all did."

"Wait, commander? The Commander of the King's Knights is here?" Aron asked, then the rest of his father's statement hit him. "And he knows about me?"

Before he could get an answer, he heard a familiar voice from behind him. Aron turned, and standing there in full armor, that did indeed gleam in the sunlight, was Devan. The knight crossed his arms, much as his father had a few minutes before, and stared at the boy for a long moment. He looked displeased. Very displeased.

"I won't sugar coat it, lad," he said. "That was a stupid and dangerous thing you did in Lanfield."

A surge of fear shot up in the boy. What did Devan think? Did he believe he'd stabbed the guard? Would he be arrested and taken to jail in Lanfield? Surely Jasmine would have told him otherwise—if she'd had a chance to talk to him.

"I didn't kill anyone," Aron said, almost pleading.

Devan snorted.

"As if I ever thought that," he said. "You are brash and impetuous, but you are no murderer."

Aron breathed a sigh of relief. Devan's cold stare softened just a bit, but not by much.

"No, as it turns out, Jarl kept your knife and put it in his own partner's gut. The two guards had been feuding for months, and he saw a good opportunity to rid himself of Harry. Once a captain of the guard finally arrived on the scene, he realized that they'd better fetch me as she demanded before they tried breaking Jasmine's door down. Jarl's story broke apart soon enough after I arrived. He stabbed Harry and concocted the story about you coming for revenge. Enough people witnessed the spectacle at the gate to back him up, and he found a few other guards eager enough to avenge one of their own to come after you. He's in the king's dungeon now and will likely never see the light again—not that he'd want to, since it seems that Harry was not quite as dead as he believed and will survive his wound after all. Both have been removed from the city guard.

"But that wasn't the stupid and dangerous part. I meant you running away. Surely you knew Jasmine would protect you until I arrived."

Aron had a terrible thought then.

"I didn't get her in trouble, did I?"

"Of course not. Jasmine is fine, though she is a bit miffed with you for leaving the way you did. You'll owe her an apology next time you see her. Now, why did you run?"

Devan's gaze had hardened again as he stared down at the boy. Aron wanted to shrink into the dirt of the road in shame.

"I was scared," he answered weakly. "The guards sounded angry, and Jarl was shouting for them to kick the door in. I thought they were going to kill me. I needed to get away."

"No one would have dared lay a hand on you," the knight answered sternly. "You were under the protection of the Commander of the King's Knights, and they all knew it."

Aron's mouth fell open at that. Wait a minute, what had he just said?

"The…commander…?"

Devan finally cracked a big smile at the confusion on the boy's face.

"Yes," he answered. "Commander Devan Kyle, at your service. Or rather, you are at mine. I can't deny that I'm disappointed. Your actions were not very worthy of a knight. We always face our problems head on. We don't run from them."

"The boy will never be a knight," his father interrupted. "He's just a farm boy. We have no riches and no history of knights in the family. Don't feed his fantasies."

Devan gave his father an appraising look and frowned. Aron hoped for a moment that the knight would correct him. Surely, he had trained him in Lanfield for a reason and intended to make him a knight all along. His heart soared. This was the moment he'd been waiting for his entire life. He was going to be trained as a knight, by the Commander of the King's Knights, no less. But he was severely disappointed.

"Probably right," Devan said, finally. His mouth twisted as he considered. "Still…well, we can't ponder it now. We've got a battle to fight."

"How will we fight them?" Aron asked.

"*We* won't be fighting anything," his father interrupted. "You will be going back to help your mother. The women and children are being sent over the mountain, and you are to go with them."

Aron was disappointed. He was not a child, not after all he'd been through in the last couple of months. He'd killed a goblin, though he had to admit to himself that it was more by accident than anything else. He knew his arguments would likely fall on deaf ears, but then...he had another thought.

"To protect them?" Aron asked hopefully. He expected that to earn his father's ire, but instead, his Da gave him a look as if re-appraising him.

"If need be."

"Do you think the goblins are going to take the village?" he asked, a tinge of fear in his voice. "Is that why you are sending the women and children away?"

"Of course not," Devan answered. "I have a hundred knights hidden in the forest outside of town. They'll strike when the time is right and take them by surprise."

"But there are thousands of goblins out there."

The knight looked at him for a moment, as if questioning how the boy had such knowledge. Then he waved the comment away dismissively.

"One of the King's Knights is worth at least a hundred goblins. It's not the monsters we have to worry about anyway. Once we take out the men who are driving them, the beasts will scatter and run."

"So, Doubloon was right," Aron said, his thoughts going back to his conversation with the dragon.

His father and the knight looked at him strangely.

"I can help..." the boy began, but they both cut him off.

"You cannot," his father said. "Commander Kyle may have taught you a few things about using a sword, but you'd be more a danger to us than the goblins, I'd wager."

"But..."

"Your father is right," Devan said. "Though you show promise, you're far too green to be on the front lines. Go and help your mother. Get her and your brothers to safety."

"But..."

He wanted to protest that he had, in fact, killed a goblin, and a wild one at that, but neither man would hear it. He wanted to tell them about Doubloon, offer the drag-on's help, but those words caught in his throat as he realized what it would mean. He stood there, mouth open, trying to find some sort of argument.

"That's enough!" his father roared. "Go help your mother now, or I'll send you there with an aching backside."

Dejected, Aron turned and shuffled slowly back toward the house, but he never made it. Once he was out of sight of the men, and they had turned their attention back to the coming battle, he changed his path and pointed himself toward the mountains. He could help, and he would help, whether Devan and his father wanted him to or not.

Twenty-One

Though Aron felt a pang of guilt at once again disobeying his father, he knew what he was about to do was right. Devan had just told him that knights don't run away from their problems, they face them head on, yet now, they wanted him to run away. He would not do it again.

He sprinted up the mountain road to the spot where Doubloon had dropped him off, but when he rounded the screening tree line, his friend was nowhere to be found. He felt a moment of panic as he searched, but in a matter of minutes, the dragon's shadow fell over him, and its great wings rustled the leaves and trees. He landed softly in the grass next to Aron, saying nothing, but giving the boy a long look, as if trying to decide what to do next.

"Doubloon," Aron began, but then his voice failed him. He thought about their conversations, what had happened to the dragon's father and mother. He realized for the first time since he'd hatched his plan the gravity of what he was about to ask his new friend.

Seeing the boy struggling for words, Doubloon lowered his head to look into Aron's eyes, and he sighed.

"I know the question you wish to ask, and I've been pondering it myself since we first flew over the goblin army," he said. "And, yes, I have decided that I will help you. Not them. You. I have hidden myself away from humans for so many years, and for good reason, but I find that I cannot abandon you and those you love."

The weight of his friend's decision hit Aron hard. The fact that the dragon would reveal himself to humankind and potentially put himself in danger to help him, meant a lot. Tears rolled down Aron's face as he realized the sacrifice his friend was about to make. He wondered, would he do the same for Doubloon? He hoped that he would. He may have to. Doubloon's history with humans was not a happy one, and he didn't know how his people might react when a myth appeared in their village. Nearly all the stories about dragons painted them as villains, and there were a lot of ways this could go wrong. Aron ran forward, wrapping his arms around the dragon's neck in the closest thing to a hug that he could give the great beast.

"Thank you," he sobbed. "Thank you."

"No," Doubloon answered. "Thank you. I believe you may have given me the greater gift."

The dragon endured the embrace for a few moments and then tried to extricate himself from the still crying boy, by pushing him away gently with one claw and raising his head.

"Now," he said with determination in his gruff voice. "I think I have some goblins to dispatch."

Aron pulled himself up to his full height, trying to look the part of the knight. He struggled to straighten his face and stop the flow of tears. If he were to be a warrior, he had to be made of stronger stuff. He walked to the dragon's side, waiting for the wing to come down so he could climb aboard. Instead, Doubloon raised the wing out of his reach. Aron looked at him in shock and betrayal.

"No," his friend said. "It's clear your family doesn't want you in harm's way, and neither do I. You have a pure soul, something rare in a human in my experience, and I don't want you involved in the ugliness that is about to happen out there. Stay here and await my return, or better yet, go and be with your family. Should the goblins manage to break through, your place is with them, to protect them as best you can."

Aron's first reaction was anger. His face flushed crimson, and he clenched his fists at his sides, preparing to argue with Doubloon. The dragon was being just like his father. He took a step toward his new friend, not sure what he was going to do, but with a burning desire to lash out at the unfairness of it all. He opened his mouth to shout something that he would likely regret later. Doubloon tilted his head, waiting for the outburst. Aron's tongue caught in his throat, though, looking at his friend who was about to go against every instinct that he had just to help. He remembered the lesson he'd learned with the guards at the gate, the disappointment that Devan and his father had shown in him. He couldn't be an angry child anymore, not if he wanted to be a knight, and not if he wanted to save his family and village.

The boy's bluster died with a large exhalation. He sagged and nodded his head, acknowledging that Doubloon was right. As much as he longed to ride the dragon's back into battle, be the hero of his village, and win his chance to be a knight, he knew that he was not prepared. He had to look no further than his battle with the goblin in the mountains to see how much he had yet to learn. What could he do from the dragon's back other than watch and be a distraction? He was no knight yet, but there was still hope.

He looked up into Doubloon's eyes and was surprised to see respect there.

"You have come far, little one," he said. "You have farther still to travel, but you are well on the path. Now, go and protect your family."

With that, the dragon gave him that toothy smile, once terrifying, that he'd come to love over the last weeks. Then, Doubloon gathered himself and launched into the sky. He zipped away toward the village.

Twenty-Two

Aron ran back down the path toward his home as he watched his friend soar overhead, revealing himself to humans for the first time in many generations. It had been so long that the people who were about to get their first glimpse of him thought his kind to be a mere legend, a tale for children. Aron scrambled to the top of a rock on the edge of the village to get a better view of the moment. The sun glinted off Doubloon's scales with even more beauty than he had ever imagined in one of the fantasies that had so often gotten him in trouble. Unlike those daydreams, this dragon wasn't coming to destroy the town or be slain by a brave shepherd boy. This monster was coming to save the village, and his family.

As Doubloon crossed over the front lines, silence fell among the men below. The cries that had echoed a moment before as the warriors prepared to defend the village, died to nothing. The goblin army, which was just now coming into view of the boy's perch, paused in its march, causing a clumsy chaos as rear lines bumped into those in front. Monsters went down in a heap, and the few humans among them rushed about shouting commands that he was too far away to hear clearly.

Then the fear and wonder that had frozen his people for a moment broke. Cries went up among the men below, and a volley of arrows shot into the air in the wake of his friend's flight.

"NO!" Aron screamed, too far away from the line to be heard. He watched in horror as the arrows sailed toward the dragon, then breathed a sigh of relief as the few that actually found their mark bounced harmlessly off Doubloon's scaly armor. The townsfolk were not finished, though. Another volley followed, and again Aron screamed unheard. He scrambled down from the rock and began to run toward the front line, heedless of the warnings of his father and Devan to stay away. He had to stop this, had to explain to them that the dragon was not part of the attacking army, but here to help.

He froze, though, as Doubloon surged suddenly upward, taking himself high enough in the sky to be well out of any arrow's reach. It was almost as if Aron felt the sudden change in the dragon's demeanor before he saw his friend's reaction. Doubloon turned toward the humans below and hovered in the sky, flapping his great wings slowly. He let out a ferocious roar of rage that shook the ground nearby. The beast staring down at Aron's home and family did not look like his friend of the last many weeks. In that moment, he looked far more like the vicious, savage monster of Aron's imagination. A shiver ran down the boy's spine as he saw the rage rise in the dragon, an emotion that up until now, he'd not thought his friend capable of. He wondered, for just a split second, if he had unwittingly brought destruction on his people. Would the dragon's mistrust of humans be more powerful than their friendship? Then, Doubloon spoke.

"ENOUGH!" he roared, his voice booming across the battlefield and echoing back off the mountains. "I come on behalf of the young one named Aron, who I am proud to call friend. Though I bear little love for humankind, he has asked me to save his family and his home, which I do out of respect for him. If you desire a quick victory, follow me. But if one more arrow is fired at me, I will leave you to your own devices and your own fate. It will not be a happy one."

Murmurs rolled through the assembled defenders, and Aron wondered for a moment how his friends and family would react to this declaration. Would they listen to the dragon or would fear win out? Would Doubloon really abandon them in his anger? The dragon didn't wait to see what the humans would decide. He wheeled in the air, and with a few strong strokes of his wings sent himself sailing out to meet the goblin army. He rose slowly as he went, and when he reached the front line of the monsters, he dove, screaming out of the clouds, straight at the attackers. The beauty of the sun on his scales that Aron had often admired became something more menacing now, more like light playing on the blade of a razor-sharp sword. He spun as he dove, the wind from his descent stirring up great dust devils among the army below. Just above the heads of the goblins, a great gout of flame shot from his open maw. It exploded against the earth, sending dirt and monsters flying into the air.

Doubloon swooped up and away from the army as spears and arrows followed weakly in his wake. He emerged from flame and dust with a struggling goblin held in each of his front claws. As he rose once more, he tossed them down among their brethren. Looking at the frightening beast now terrorizing the enemy, he could hardly believe that it was the good-natured creature that he had come to call friend. Aron didn't want to watch after that initial attack, but he stood transfixed, unable to look away. He felt relieved that the dragon had not allowed him to ride into battle. He would only have slowed Doubloon down, and he now understood the truth of what he'd been told. He really didn't want to be in the middle of what was happening to the goblin army. Even from this distance, he felt a little queasy as he watched the destruction being rained down on them. He had to remind himself more than once that the goblins would have done the same things, or worse, to his friends and family.

Again and again, the dragon dove toward the enemy. Gouts of flame scorched through monster and human alike, leaving a swath of smoking destruction in his wake with each pass. The enemy's front lines now rushed around in chaos and panic, not knowing how to respond to this new horror. What they thought would be an easy victory over a small, unprepared village had become a death trap. Their handlers lost control of the situation, and the monsters collided with each other, and in some cases, even attacked each other as they tried desperately to scramble away from the fiery rain of death falling from the sky.

As the confusion grew and the ranks began to separate, Aron heard a whooping cry go up from the village and saw Devan's knights come galloping full stride out of their hiding place in the forest. The gleam of their armor was almost as impressive as the show put on by the dragon's scales, a great lance of shining light driving straight into the heart of darkness.

The knights, with Devan at the forefront Aron was almost certain, leaped into the nearest breach created by the dragon's attacks. They hacked and slashed to the sides of their horses, beating back the remaining goblins and riding others down as they aimed arrow-like straight for the knot of human soldiers at the middle of the army. At that point, the men in the enemy ranks also lost their nerve. Most of them broke and ran alongside the monsters that were now in full flight. A brave, or stupid, few stood their ground as the knights rode them down. Swords clashed in the field outside the village, but only briefly. The ragged band of men, broken by the terror of Doubloon's attacks, were no match for Devan's well-oiled unit of warriors.

Doubloon continued to harry the retreating armies, dipping and diving. He held his fiery breath in check now that the knights were on the field, not wanting to accidentally torch allies. Instead, he dove low over the heads of the goblins and men, unleashing deafening roars that sent them scattering or falling to their knees in terror. Occasionally, he plucked up one of the monsters and tossed it high into the air, adding to the fear as it plummeted back to earth among the crowd of its allies.

The battle proved brief with the dragon leading the way, and it was a rout. Within minutes of the first sword clash, the few remaining men who had driven the goblins toward the village had been unhorsed and surrounded by the King's Knights. Those who hadn't stood their ground and been captured were in full flight, along with the monsters they commanded.

Doubloon followed the fleeing and scrambling army

until they were well away from the village, then he pulled up. He let out another ear-splitting roar at the retreating enemies and blasted a huge fountain of flame into the air above him for good measure. If their foes could possibly run faster, they did. Then he spoke again, in a thunderous voice enhanced by his magic to make sure that every person and monster on both sides of the line would clearly hear.

"Know that the young one Aron, his people, and his village are under my protection," he roared. "Return here at your peril."

As silence fell on the battlefield, a great cheer rose from the human side of the line.

Twenty-Three

As soon as Doubloon issued his threat over the heads of the fleeing army, and he heard the rousing shouts and cheers go up from his own people, Aron remembered where he was supposed to be. He shook off his fascination with what he'd just witnessed and ran toward his home.

He pulled up short at the edge of the village as he met the women and children who were already making their way along the road to Lanfield. As the cheers and celebration continued from the front line, they turned back toward the battle. Those who had remained in their homes ventured out into the dirt roads to see what the clamor was about. The threat gone, the men of the village rushed back to find their families, and a great celebration broke out in the streets between the homes. Families hugged, cried, and cheered as they reunited with loved ones who they'd feared only a few moments before they might never see again. Instead of the expected disaster, the battle had been won, and not a single man of the village had even needed to lift a sword.

Aron pushed his way through the crowd, seeking his own family in the uproar. As they came into view, his father opened his arms and enveloped him in a great hug. He lifted the boy off the ground and swung him around, planting kisses on his face, which shocked Aron. Before the battle, his father had been angry and promised that he would pay for his foolishness, but his greeting now was completely different. Aron had never seen his father act this way, and certainly had never seen him this happy and proud.

He returned a thoroughly confused Aron to the ground, kneeling to look him in the eye. For a second, his Da almost looked ashamed, but that disappeared quickly.

"It seems that I owe you an apology," he said. "I believe one of your fantasies has just saved our lives."

Tears ran down his father's face as he hugged Aron again, uncomfortably hard.

"Careful, there, don't break anything," Devan said from behind them. "After all, I can't have him injured when he takes the field to begin his training."

Aron spun around then, looking hopefully into the knight's smiling face.

"You mean…"

"I did say that there was precedent for accepting someone who had performed great acts of heroism, didn't I?" Devan said. "I believe this qualifies. I will, of course, need to get the blessing of King James to make it official, but I think that he'll be much more amenable once he hears the story that our prisoners have to tell."

The boy ran to the knight and grabbed him in an

awkward hug around his armored waist. The knight stood for a second, speechless and a bit uncomfortable. Then he pushed the boy away.

"Here now, you may yet be a knight one day," he said. "And I am your commanding officer. Some decorum, please."

Aron stepped back quickly, looking around confused. Then the knight gave him a wink and a smile, ruffled the boy's hair, and pulled him close again.

"I'll make an exception in this situation," he said with a laugh.

Aron looked at his father and then to his mother and brothers, who were staring in stunned silence. He ran immediately to his mother, hugging her, bubbling with joy at the news he'd just received.

"I'm going to be a knight," he spluttered. "Sir Devan says that he will train me…"

He trailed off when he met his mother's eyes and saw the shimmering tears and deep sadness there. He had just returned home after having been missing for weeks. He realized they may have even believed he was dead. And here he was, preparing to leave them again, and thrilled to do it. He realized suddenly how selfish his joy at that was and how it must seem to his family and felt a pang of shame. His joy faded and his smile slipped as he turned back to Devan.

"Do you think I could have a few weeks at least to visit with my family before we go back to Lanfield to begin my training?" he asked sheepishly. "It's been a long time since I've seen them, and I have some things to make up to them."

Devan smiled wider.

"You can take as much time as you want with them," he said. "Because you won't be going back to Lanfield, at least not right away."

Aron's eyes widened in confusion.

"But how will I train?"

"Well, in convincing King James to send us to help put the goblin army down, I also planted the seed with him that the lands north of the mountain still needed the king's protection and were still worthy of it," Devan said. "He has authorized me to establish a new contingent of knights here, the Knights of the North.

"That, of course, means there will eventually have to be a commander. Protector of the North, I believe the King decided to call the position. I've convinced him to leave it vacant for the time being, until someone might prove himself worthy of the title. My second, Gareth, will serve in that capacity until such time as someone is chosen, and he will oversee your training."

The boy turned back to his family, beaming. It was the best of all worlds for him. He would be a knight, and he would be home.

"You will, of course, have to report to me in Lanfield so that I can measure your progress and test your skills," Devan continued. "And when you're older, you will have to live there for a time for your formal training in the ways of the knighthood, but that will be a few years away yet. For now, I imagine you have quite the story to tell, and I'm guessing everyone here will want to hear it. I would certainly like to hear it."

The boy looked around at the eager faces of those within earshot of the knight's speech. They all had questions. Out of the corner of his eye, he caught a glint of sun off scale in the skies at the southern end of the village. Doubloon, largely forgotten in the human celebration, was slowly winging his way back toward his home in the mountains.

"Not yet," Aron said, breaking away from friends and family and running up the road behind the dragon.

He scrambled through the streets of the village as fast as he could. Twisting and turning to avoid the people who constantly tried to stop him to congratulate him, thank him, or give him a slap on the back. It seemed he was finally the hero that he had always dreamed of being, but the true hero—his friend—was becoming smaller and smaller in the distance. The dragon seemed lonely and sad in his flight, and it broke Aron's heart.

Finally, he pulled free of the press of people and barreled up the path toward the mountain, crying his friend's name, but the dragon paid no heed. By the time he reached the field where they had first landed in the village, Aron realized that he was not going to catch up. He stopped and sent out a cry within his mind.

Doubloon, he thought toward his friend. *Please come back.*

The dragon's flight paused, and slowly he turned. A few minutes later, the wind from Doubloon's wings ruffled the boy's hair as his friend settled down in front of him.

"I thought you'd be enjoying your hero's celebration," the dragon said. Aron could hear the hint of sadness in his voice. It was something he'd never heard from the dragon before. "You deserve it."

"I didn't do anything," Aron argued. "It was all you. You sent the goblins running. You allowed the knights to capture the humans who were driving it. You did it all."

"You did much more than you give yourself credit for," Doubloon said with a chuckle.

"Why don't you come back to the village with me?" the boy asked. "I could introduce you to everyone. I know they'd love to meet you. You'd be a hero, too."

The dragon raised his eyes and looked back toward the celebration. Aron thought he saw a little bit of longing in that stare, but it was gone quickly as his friend shook his head.

"No, I don't think so," he said sadly. "You, little friend, have given me much hope that maybe one day dragons and humans might live peacefully together. But I don't think today is that day, for my own faults as much as theirs. You have, as you promised, given me your protection, in a manner of speaking. I'm grateful for that."

"But I didn't protect you," Aron protested. "You're the one that protected me, that protected all of us. My village, my family, would probably be gone without you."

"That's true," the dragon answered. "But thanks to you, little brother, they're my family now, too."

The acknowledgement that Doubloon felt that way about him sent tears streaming down the boy's cheeks once again.

"So, I'll see you again, then?"

"Of course," Doubloon answered, almost as though offended by the question. Then he smiled.

"I have a gift for you," the dragon said. He reached a claw back beneath his left wing and did something Aron couldn't see. "I didn't know if I was going to give it to you yet, but I believe you deserve it."

When Doubloon's talon came forward again, a golden amulet dangled from one outstretched claw. It was round, about the size of the boy's hand, with the likeness of a dragon's face stamped into the metal.

"It's beautiful," Aron said, carefully taking the medallion and holding it up for a better look. Inset into the back was a small red jewel.

"It's from my hoard," Doubloon said. "But it's more than that. At the center of the amulet, encased in gold, is one of my sire's scales. It is the last thing that I have of him."

"I can't take this," Aron said, trying to give it back to his friend. "It's the only thing you have to remember your father by."

The dragon refused to accept it.

"You can, and you will," he said. "Dragons do not offer gifts from their hoard lightly, and I would be greatly offended if you refused it.

"The amulet will offer you protection. Keep it secret. Keep it safe. Should you ever need me, all you need to do is call. Through that, no matter how far I am, I will hear, and I will come."

Doubloon looked back to the village, and Aron followed his gaze. A few people had become braver and were starting to slowly venture toward them.

"Now, I believe it is time for me to go," the dragon said. "Remember our friendship and never forget your dreams. Fare you well, Aron…for the moment, at least."

The boy tried to say something, tried to convince his friend to stay and meet his people. But he saw in the dragon's eyes that was not to be, not yet, anyway. His voice caught in his throat, and he stood mutely as Doubloon launched himself into the air and began to spiral slowly upward.

"I'll see you soon," Aron shouted to him, finally finding his voice.

"I am sure you will," came the answer, and then Doubloon was heading homeward.

As he soared away toward the mountains, the people from the village finally caught up to Aron. He was swept away in a cacophony of congratulations, handshakes, pats on the back, and questions. They cheered the boy and hoisted him up on their shoulders, carrying him toward his home.

High above the celebration, in the clouds, a single tear fell from the eye of a great golden dragon.

The adventures of Aron and Doubloon will continue...

Dubloon says goodbye.